HUNTED is the second boc  and follows directly on fror is available as a paperback to purchase from Amazon or to download from the Kindle Store.

PROLOGUE

They stood in the dock.

Stoic awaiting their fate.

The jury had taken all but an hour to come to their conclusion.

The foreman of the jury stands and delivers their verdict.

"We find the defendant guilty your Honour."

***

Paedophile – noun (C) UK (US paedophile) someone who is sexually interested in children

Josephine - Late Summer 1981

I remember the day that I found out that there was actual terminology for what he was. He was obviously a monster, but he was also a paedophile. That was a shock in itself, but what I found even more disturbing, was that there were more of them. An abundance of evil monsters who thought nothing of taking what wasn't theirs. An innocence; a childhood that could never be repaired or regained. Without even a second thought, they shattered lives. They were a disease and I decided that I would be the cure.

Josephine

I was 16, nearly 17 years old. The past had happened there was no changing it. I decided that I could not, and would not be a victim.... or rather, my mother had. She'd always engrained in me that there were far worse off people. "Count your blessings, Josephine..."

Anyway, it was my week's work experience, and it had been arranged for Clarks Court in the City. It was the Barristers Chambers for John Allott Abrahams QC. A Silk and renowned defence barrister, always willing to take on the underdog. Mother, she couldn't help but pass comment if she ever saw him on the television. He would be stood outside the courts and making a statement of how the jury had made the right decision, justice served etc., etc... and she'd pipe up... "Well, you know they've done it if they've got him representing them... How does he even sleep at night?"

I never really understood what she was talking about to be honest. I just got used to her continual rants at the telly and her passing comment. Dad's chair now sat empty. He was no longer present to counter or curb her bitterness, which was made worse by his premature departure.

My work experience choice, well, I say choice very loosely as I did not have one. It had absolutely no link to my lifelong aspirations, and in fact, as a teenager I really didn't know what I wanted to do when I grew up. I was pretty sure however, that I had absolutely no interest in the law, nor becoming a solicitor, or barrister or whatever you were when you dressed up in robes and put on a curly white wig. Nevertheless, I went as the school had arranged it and more importantly, Mum had told me that I had to go.

I was up early on the Tuesday morning and I walked to the end of the street. It had seemed strange not starting on the Monday, but I'd been told that they'd be too busy to deal with me at the start of the week. I don't really recall what month it was, but it must have been very late August or early September, as I do remember the chill of the morning air, the condensation on our neighbour's car windscreen and the daddy longlegs that were milling about.

I stood at the end of the street waiting for Sharon and Tony to walk past. I was to join them for their daily commute. Sharon and Tony were friends of Mum and Dad's from years back. They lived locally and had agreed to show me the commuting ropes. Mum had mentioned in passing about me going up to the City and Sharon had offered. As I looked out for them, I stood there idly with my arms wrapped around me, trying to keep myself warm in the early morning chill. At that time, I had absolutely no idea just how life-changing that week's work experience would really be. It would give me insight, and ultimately my overall purpose in life.

Superintendent Jo Gordon

After my initial panic had subsided, I focused on what I had been given, and I realised that it didn't mean a thing. The female who had dropped off the bag of goodies didn't leave her name. There was no clear chain of evidence; and what really did her pages of notes, the knife and photo really prove? For all I knew, it could have been an elaborate ploy on "her" part to get the conviction overturned. She was certainly clever enough.

Obviously, I did due diligence and I tried to trace and locate her. However, I came up empty-handed. The CCTV in the front office was grainy. There was no clear facial image, and my trawl of the local CCTV and ANPR cameras revealed absolutely nothing of her identity. I wasn't being underhand or untrue, but I really didn't feel the need to disclose this supposed 'new evidence'.

After all, what really was it? There was no real provenance and I'd already ridden the most horrendous of shit storms. Case after case being reviewed, simply due to her name being somewhere in the file. No, I decided now was not the time to reopen Pandora's box.

Josephine

I didn't look like the established teenager that I was. Nope, the fringe framing my face meant that an outsider, would probably estimate my age as barely 13 years old. Even wearing makeup and a short skirt, I would never be able to pass as an eighteen-year-old. Not that it was even a concern for me as I had no friends. No one wanted me to hang out with them. There was no danger of my conning my way past a bouncer. My youth practically radiated, and I think forevermore I would hear the phrase "Got any ID love?"

Therefore, whilst on work experience even though I had borrowed Sharon's dark green silk ruffled blouse and a pair of her black tailored trousers, I still looked every bit a child. I remember that first day so vividly, especially the rat-run that was Bank Underground Station and my nervous navigation of the various exits. When I finally found the right one, it really was a light at the end of the tunnel moment.

I emerged into the morning sunshine and having taken this turn and that, I finally got to my destination; a Dickensian building which stood grandly before me.

I walked through the blue-painted front door and I was greeted by what I considered at the time to be a rather scruffy man. His suit teamed with a matching waistcoat (and although clearly expensive), did not suit his unkempt appearance of stubble and untamed hair. This man however, I later discovered was the Clerk and a rather important man in the Chambers. He practically ran the place.

Shelley

In those early days they kept me separated. Anyone associated with the police, in prison is instantly hated. Although I was never an officer, and my time served with the Force had been a flash in the pan; to the other residents, I was still seen as the enemy. I was a pig, and for that I was instantly despised and fair game for a beating.

John

Life has suddenly become complex and full of contradictions. I had always seen everything as black and white. Right and wrong. Good and bad. After all, that was what made me become a Copper in the first place. Ironic really because my one constant, and the institution that defined me as a person, has ultimately turned its back on me. It disregarded my loyalty and good service and in one deadly blow, it destroyed both me and my family.

I had never wanted to be, and certainly never expected to be a single parent, breadwinner and latterly a committed lobbyist for justice. I had joined the countless number of convicted criminal's loved ones who championed their family member's innocence, whose main focus and campaign were to have them set free, and oh boy was it draining.

Josephine

The Clerk; I discovered was called Robbie. Full name: Robert James Ball. He was the main man around the Chambers. He organised who did what. He got the cases, compiled the notes, and he told the barristers where they needed to be and who they'd represent. And the reason why he looked so dishevelled on my first day? Well, he'd been out the night before wining and dining a solicitor in order to win the next big case. Getting pissed with solicitors and dealing with the associated hangover the next day, was probably the most important part of his job.

Robbie seemed a rather angry and aggressive type. By his demeanour, it was clear that he had no real time for me, and it made me wonder as to why he'd agreed to me going there in the first place. He set out the "rules" as he put it. He had decided that I was to get a real experience of the Chambers.

"You'll be working from the bottom up". He said this with a fierce grin whilst handing me his coffee cup and pointing me over to the kitchen. "You'll start now and I'll have a black coffee, three sugars and make sure you wash the cup".

Shelley

To say that I found prison life easy would be a lie. I remember so well that first dreadful moment when I stepped through the gated entrance, and my goodness the stench, it just hit me. It was strong; a mixture of stale cigarettes, body odour and desperation.

I tried my best to just get on with things. I was given advice by a youngish Officer at my 'Prison Briefing' as he put it... He explained about the processes and procedures (all the formal stuff) and then he gave me the survival talk. He told me that I would be kept separately due to my links with the police, but there would be some interaction with the other segregated prisoners. We were all there on that wing because we had been assessed as vulnerable, and this he had explained was for a variety of reasons.

Clearly quite well-rehearsed, his speech mainly concentrated on me keeping my head down. "Remember this one thing. No one gets killed for saying nothing!" His words rang out, and I realised just how big a mess I was actually in. He went on to the day-to-day things like I'd get a minimum of 30 minutes a day exercise and I would have daily access to the shower, etc., etc ... But to be honest I didn't really take any of it in. I knew that the long bubble baths that I was used to, and the mood lighting provided by a flickering candle were a thing of the past. Although I didn't really expect anything different. I was, after all, now in prison.

***

I got nowhere near the 30 minutes of daily exercise that I was promised. They were understaffed and just couldn't supervise everyone. It was the norm. Like everywhere these days, they over-promised and under-delivered. It was horrendous. My anxiety had really peaked, and I knew I needed the exercise to give me some form of control. I did ask for a little more time however, this fell on deaf ears. No one seemed to hear or even care. It was just the same when I said I didn't do it. No one heard me. When I said I was struggling, they just didn't listen. They made the assumption I was guilty and that was that. I was now in the system and I just had to get on with it.

Josephine

I quickly got to understanding the workings of the Chambers, and my role there. I made coffee after coffee and I did a lot of paper shredding. I also spent a lot of my time in small dusty cupboards, surrounded by files secured with pink cotton ribbon, searching for this case-file or that…. and once Robbie had no more uses for me in the Chambers, he would then send me over to the Bailey, and I would sit in the public gallery listening to the cases.

The first one that I sat in on was a murder case. I was fascinated. More so because that very morning, I had made coffee for the five suspects sat in the dock. They had been laughing and joking. They were carefree and certainly never gave me any insight as to why they needed the services of a Barrister.

The case was a gang (they were the gang), who had chased the victim through the deprived streets of South London. He had been to the area to visit his Nan and on leaving the block, he had dissed (disrespected) them. This had apparently signed his death warrant. They chased him like a pack of wolves. They hunted him down. Pursuing him through the streets and alleyways, before finally cornering him at the railway sidings. They had stabbed him multiple times and they left him there to die. Witnesses had observed them walking away after the act; describing them as laughing and joking and nonchalant in their behaviour. I could not believe how callous they were, and how little regard that they had for his innocence or his life. That young boy had been to visit his sick grandmother, and rather like the fairy-tale of Little Red Riding Hood, he too had fallen foul of the wolf.

Superintendent Jo Gordon

What is a girl to do when she is newly promoted and very much needing to make her mark in the world? Do you remember DC Rachel Cooper? The Officer who made the breakthrough with the Body in the Wood case? Well... after her sitting her Sergeants exams and passing with flying colours, I asked her where she wanted to be?

When she sat opposite me at this very desk, I had expected her to say a position within the Flying-Squad, or to ask for a secondment to the NCA. I would have pulled all the strings, and got her to wherever she'd wanted to be. Rewarding all her good work etc. But, do you know what she actually said? "Ma'am, I would like a role within Cold Cases, please..." Bloody Cold Cases! I personally cannot think of anything more boring, and or less rewarding. They are cold for a reason. We have NO LEADS. There is no budget, and so long as it's not one of my cases (which of course there are none) … I really couldn't give a rat's arse about any other sloppy underperforming detective's case. Yes, I know there is still a victim without closure. A suspect living on borrowed time but it's the Lead Detective's lookout to solve it, and not mine. Well, so long as it's not on the Press' and/ or Senior Management's radar that is! That lot, they do love to flap and declare a critical incident!

Josephine

So, there I am sat listening to the Forensic Scientist - The Prosecution's Expert Witness. They are advising of who was likely to have been holding the knife, at the time of the fatal blow. They had surmised this from the direction of the blood splatter on both the victim's and suspect's clothing. It was fascinating stuff.

I was thoroughly absorbed, but then there is an objection from the Defence Barrister (our side). Although rather slight, he still manages to project his voice well. Both parties are called up to the Judge for some whispering. It is decided that due to a point of law, there needs to be an adjournment whilst clarification is sought. It is almost lunchtime and it's clear that the rather elderly Judge is struggling to keep awake, so it is decided that we will break for the day and come back again tomorrow. Tomorrow?! I observed the very strange timekeeping in court. It is no wonder that some court cases can drag on for months, if they break for the day so very easily... Anyway, I leave the court and I make my way over to the Chambers. I see Robbie on my way back in.

"You OK kid?". He says.
"Yes fine, it's fascinating!" I enthused. My tone evidently highlighting this.
"Ah good, well you can get off now if you like. I heard that the case is adjourned for the day and I've got nothing for you here. To be honest, afternoons are my busiest time and the phones always go crazy after four." My face drops, and on seeing my disappointment, he says...
"Well, there is Court Number Three? A paedophile case that is continuing this afternoon. Do you fancy that?"
"Umm ok, great, I'll sit in on that one..." I say this smiling back at him.

"Ok, if you are sure. It might not be very nice. Just see what you think, and if you don't like it, you can get off home and I'll see you tomorrow".

I had absolutely no idea what a paedophile case was, but I was pretty sure it couldn't have been as unpleasant as a murder.

I ate the ham and pickle sandwiches that my mother had prepared for me. It was lovely just sitting there in the square at the front of the building. It was a little pocket of green that was surrounded by the high walls. After I had finished my lunch, I was beginning to feel nervous and full of anticipation, and on checking my watch, I knew it was time to make my way over to Court Number Three...

After all of my initial dread and reservations, I had actually decided that work experience was fun!

Shelley

Things are getting quite desperate for me. My paranoia and anxiety are going through the roof. I have constant pain in my chest and back, and my heart palpitations rarely stop. I try to explain this to John, telling him how I'm feeling. He is sat opposite me at today's visit, but I can tell that he is not listening. He had left the girls at home with my mum, and he was telling me that Maggie had started to wet the bed. He couldn't work out why, so he has put it down to the prison visits; saying to me... "It's unsettling for them, you know". I didn't respond. I just thought to myself, "Oh is it now? I hadn't realised!"

Of course, I knew it might have an effect, and I don't want him bringing the girls here if it's impacting on them. My role, even locked up in this place is to protect them. He made me feel such a failure and I wanted to keep them safe, do the best by them, but I also knew that I needed them. They kept me in the present.

I'm trying to help myself and to control my utter desperation, but it's so hard. Also, without being able to off-load properly on to John; today had turned into just another one of my difficult days. I try to stay positive, so I have put in for the Family Day Ballot. I'm probably being silly, pinning all of my hopes on it but I need a focus. The Governor apparently brought them in last year. They are designed to improve the behaviour amongst the inmates, to keep us connected with the outside world, and preventing us from becoming institutionalised. It sounds fabulous as there are to be inflatables, as well as hotdog and popcorn stands, hook a duck etc... The works! It's like a mini funfair that they host in the prison grounds. We would get some proper family time – all of us together. Don't get me wrong I'm not really complaining. The family room where our visits usually take place is nice enough. It doesn't have the rancid smell (that the rest of this place exudes) and I do get a cup of tea and a biscuit whilst I am sat with the girls. However, it's by no means homely and does nothing to take away my trapped and claustrophobic feelings.

Josephine

So, I go back into the Bailey and I make my way into Court Number Three. I see one of our Chamber's Barristers.   She is stood over to the left of me and is talking to a male in his mid to late 30's. She looks so smart in her navy pinstripe dress-suit, along with her robes and wig. She sees me and does a double-take. She leaves the male and she makes her way over to me. She is very assertive in her tone as she says...

"Should you really be in here?" Did Robbie send you?"
"Yes, he did. The last case that I was sat in on has been adjourned for the day."
"And did he tell you what type of case it was?"
"Yes, I'm fully aware." I try to say this with authority.
"Well, you look rather young to be sat in here, it could be rather distressing."

"I know I look young, but I am 18." – As I lie to her, I can feel myself instantly blushing, and I am hoping that she doesn't notice.

"Ok then, if you are sure? Lucky old you in having such a youthful complexion."

She leaves me and goes back over to the male who is still stood in the dock.

A few minutes later, the Jury shuffle in. I study each one of them. It amazes me that they have the power in their hands to decide the fate of this man. It is down to them to decide if he should be punished. I am daydreaming slightly as the Clerk then instructs us to "All Rise" in response to the Judge's arrival from his Chambers. Robotically we all do as asked, and then we settle back down and the afternoon proceedings begin. The Prosecution then call their first witness to the stand.

Superintendent Jo Gordon

So, I get DC Cooper into her newly appointed DS role, within the Cold Cases Department. She is working alongside DI Kevin Smart. I am not overly keen on Smart as he used to be in the DPS (Department of Professional Standards), and sometimes I think that he's forgotten that he is no longer there. He has got too caught up in the idea that all cops are bad, rather than seeing that sometimes it is necessary to act in a certain way.

My view is still and always will be, that the end justifies the means. Sadly, however, I am one of a dying breed in this place. Officially, I toe the party line but politics and me are not the best of friends. I am here to get a job done and if I offend someone in the process, they really do need to grow a pair and just get on with it.

The Police over the years has become diluted. No longer can you actually police. You know, clip the little buggers around the ear so that they know instantly that they have done wrong. No, not these days, these days, we also need to get involved with the root-cause, be social workers and their friends. Well… it's not really their fault is it?! It's society that has failed them. We wouldn't want to criminalise the little darlings…. I mean, don't get me started with the preference to "invite" the said suspect into the police station and for them to tell us as to why they robbed Mrs Miggins. Human rights these days, can prevent their instant arrest…. and heaven forfend that we give them bail conditions. No, we have to release them under investigation. Ridiculous!! Unfortunately, there is not a lot I can really do. I just do what I can, even with one of my hands tied behind my back!

John

This week's visit was just so hard. She looks so gaunt. I asked if she was eating. She nodded, but I know that she's not. I can see it. I try to listen to how she's feeling but it's hard for me too. I feel under so much pressure; she's pinning all of her hopes on me. The first thing she asks is how the appeal is getting on. I put on my best smile, and I tell her that things are moving in the right direction. The truth is however, I've got nothing new. I can't see a way to discredit the evidence against her. As tenuous as it was, and as however circumstantial, the Jury still found it compelling enough to convict. I need something concrete to prove that she did not do this.

I also had to tell her that I wasn't bringing the girls in to see her anymore. I know that she looks forward to it, but both her mum and I agree. It's not doing them any good. Maggie is bed-wetting and that is so out of character and Heidi; well, she is just so angry. She lashes out at me, Maggie, anyone. I have already been up to the school twice. The parents just stare at me. I know what they are thinking "Like mother, like daughter".... But it's not true she didn't do this.

Jo has absolutely no idea what she has done to me and my family. She was like a dog with a bone, and I'm not even sure if she cared that she got the right person. All that mattered to her was that she got someone. Case closed; job done! She's always been the same. She hates not getting results. Well, she got her result this time; but she's also destroyed me in the process. Cold-hearted bitch!

Josephine

So, through a series of questions answered by this girl, (I can't see her face clearly from where I'm sat, but I can tell by her voice that she is young) I get to realise exactly what this case is about, and exactly why the barrister was so concerned about me sitting in. As the realisation hits me, my lunchtime sandwiches begin to rise up and back into my throat. I just about make it out of the courtroom, as I vomit almost immediately into a nearby bin. I don't realise what it is at first and I don't understand what is happening to me... Panic attack? Shock maybe? A mixture of both? But I begin to sweat and I feel shaky, and then the room goes black.

Superintendent Jo Gordon

I've just finished a telecon with the Chief Super. He had called to congratulate me on reducing the Borough's robbery and burglary figures. We were getting an absolute battering, so I tasked CID to get it sorted. DI Yates is fantastic. He is well into his 30 years' service and he still has a police house in Swiss Cottage, and a couple of kids. He is going nowhere just yet. Even with his lump sum, I very much doubt he'd have enough to buy in the area. It suits me however, that he is sticking around. He is old-school and he gets the job done.

I'm pleased to hear that I am being noticed from above and that my flock are performing. I begin to think about how I'm going to reward them for their efforts. A piss up funded by moi perhaps? My thoughts however are interrupted by a sudden knock at the door. I quickly glanced down at my diary to make sure I'd not missed a meeting. Thankfully there was nothing noted.

"Come!" I say. My voice suitably authoritarian.

The heavy door is pushed open and I can see that it's the newly promoted DS Cooper.

"Ah…lovely to see you, Rachel. Come in, come in. How are you getting on?" I am genuinely pleased to see her as I view her as my protégé. We have the same drive and determination; you know the type…. She won't let things go.

"Ma'am, are you busy? Can I have a word?"

"No, not busy. I'm just nipping up to the canteen for a coffee. Do you want to join me?"

"Um well, I think what I've got to say is better said in here, Ma'am."

"Sounds ominous…. Spit it out then."

"Well Ma'am, you know the Body in the Wood job?

"Yes Rachel, what about it?"

"Well, *(she takes a sharp intake of breath)* I think there are more victims."

"Really? What do you mean? Where?"

"Well… there are three jobs over the past 35 years that I have been revisiting and, well they are the exact same MO."

"Same MO? Do enlighten me."

"Well… you know …. body burned and fingers and toes removed, teeth, etc."

"Ok and you think these are all attributed to Shelley Jones, do you?"

"Well, I don't know, but they do seem to be too an exact copy to be anything else."

"Ok, what are the dates?"

"This is the worrying part. The first one dates back to the early to mid-1980's."

Smiling back at DS Cooper and slightly mocking her in my tone... I reply... " You do realise how silly you are sounding. Jones would have been a child, a baby. It's not even remotely possible."

"No Ma'am, it's not. So, you see my concern and why I didn't want to discuss this in the open forum of the canteen."

"So, what exactly are you saying Rachel?"

"Ma'am, do you think she was telling the truth? Are we sure she did it?"

I take a deep breath; I can hear what she is saying but my brain is beginning to fog... Of course, she bloody did it. My stomach then flips as I remember the bag of disregarded "evidence" that is still stuffed in my desk drawer.

"Ok Rachel. Let's not be hasty. This is all theory, no actual evidence one way or the other. Slow up a bit and revisit every job, and then we'll have a proper discussion."

"Well…. Ma'am, that is what I have been doing...."

"Look, Rachel!" I say a little more harshly than I meant to. Softening my tone, I start again. "Rachel, I need some time to look at this. Thank you for bringing it to my attention, but we'll do this properly. There is no reason to jump to conclusions. Leave it with me for now. Oh, and Rachel, don't discuss this with anyone else. OK?"

Rachel looks over at me, nodding her head, "OK, Ma'am, I'll leave it with you."

"Are those the case files?"   I ask as I have seen that she has a number of files tucked underneath her arm.

"Yes, Ma'am."

"Ok, lovely. I'll take them now."

Reluctantly and awkwardly, she unfolds her arms as she hands the case files to the Superintendent.

"Thanks, Rachel, and I'll be in touch once I have looked these over ….   Keep up the good work in the Cold Cases. I hear that DI Smart has been very impressed with what he has seen so far."

Rachel leaves my office...   What the hell?!

Shelley

I have been keeping myself busy. I went to the prison library at the beginning of the week and I practically cleared the shelves of books. I am only supposed to take one at a time, but I am such a quick reader that the librarian OK'd it that I could take more. I have really got into thrillers of late. You know the type of story that takes you down one narrative, only for the twist to make you question your whole thought process. I kinda attribute these types of books to my own life. I was merrily going down one path and then by a cruel twist of fate, I end up in here.

I have a really good feeling about the ballot. I cannot wait to see my babies. I think they just need a "normal" day with their Mummy. John had mentioned to me that the kids were not coping, but he had clearly sugar-coated it. When Mum visited, she accidentally told me that Heidi is now prone to violent outbursts.

Apparently, John has been called into the school by the Head and there have been two occasions where she has actually hurt other kids. I hardly believe it. Not my baby. She wouldn't even hurt an ant. I lost count the number of times last summer that she called me out to the paddling pool, for me to rescue a drowning bee or fly that had accidentally fallen in. All of this is killing me. I should be with them and not locked up. It's all so unfair.

Josephine

I woke up alone in the corridor on the other side of the courtroom door. I felt horrendous. I had never fainted before; it was certainly a first. My mouth was dry, so I got myself up and made my way into the toilets. They were not as I would have expected for such a grand building. In fact, they were really rather shabby; and the damp musty smell instantly caught my throat, making me gag. I splashed my face with water at the sink but it had little effect in making me feel better. I certainly wasn't well enough to return to the courtroom. I kept mulling the realisation over and over again in my mind…. There were more of them. More like him and they were called Paedophiles.

I walked down the stairs and out of the building and into the fresh air. It made me feel slightly better, but I had decided against going back to the Chambers. It was late in the day and I didn't think Robbie would really welcome my return. So, I made my way home.

I didn't say anything to Mum when I got in. She asked me if I had had a good day. I simply nodded my head and told her that I was tired and needed an early night. "I bet you do, it's a change all this commuting. I've made you a pie. It's just in the oven, give me a minute and I'll dish up."

I played with the pie on my plate, I didn't much feel like eating. The day's events had really taken its toll and they had made me think about the past. I couldn't stop myself. All I could think about was HIM.

Josephine

The next day I was up bright and early. I had a restless night but rather than feel tired, I felt energised! I had a strong desire to know more. As I stood on that street corner, I was full of anticipation and I couldn't stop myself from fidgeting, whilst I waited impatiently for Sharon and Tony to arrive.

"Morning love!" said Sharon.

"So how was it? I thought we would have seen you on the way home… not much to this work experience really. Tuesday starts, early finishes…. I'd like to work there myself!!" Sharon said this laughing. I knew she was making a joke and I should have made more of an effort to laugh, but I could only just manage to crinkle my lips to show a slight smile…. I was just eager to get going and I couldn't be bothered with her small talk.

"OK, too early for you? … I'll leave you be; you can have a nap on the train and we'll wake you up when we get there."

I walked with a purpose alongside them, and up the steep hill to the station. I had my uniform on of tailored trousers but this time, I had teamed them with a shirt and my mum's best jacket. It was the one that she would usually wear for church, but she had allowed me to borrow it. It dwarfed me slightly, but I understood that money was tight and as I was only needing to look smart for four days, there was no point in wasting money.

The train journey took no time at all. As soon as it seemed that we had got on the train, we were already there. It's amazing how if your mind is occupied, you don't notice how long things take, and my young mind was definitely occupied. I needed to know the outcome of the case at Court Number Three. I had to be sure that the monster was locked up and punished for what he had done.

Superintendent Jo Gordon

I carefully studied every one of the files that Rachel had given to me and yes, I could see that she might think that there was a link, but how could there be? There was no doubting that Shelley was meeting him that day, and no doubting that she had the means. Yes, motive was a little sketchy but she was a foundling, and quite possibly she had been expecting a welcome with open arms. Maybe she just hadn't got the reception that she felt entitled to. It was clear that the pair were related. The DNA and the science didn't lie.

I pulled out the carrier bag that the mysterious female had dropped off, and I re-read what she had provided. It made reference to mistaken identity and that it was in retaliation. However, none of what was written in that confession, bullshit or whatever it was, made any reference to the fact that she had done it before. For all I knew she was probably some crackpot that had somehow got hold of some classified info, and made up the rest of the story to fit. Yes, I suppose I should have sent off the knife to forensics, but the more I thought about it, it really did feel like a case of her or me. I would definitely be investigated if there was even a sniff of me withholding any evidence. I had to make this go away. I have not given my whole life over to the police, for her to come and take it from me. She had already taken my John and she wasn't having my career as well. I needed to bury this.

Shelley

It was weird really and totally unexpected. The DC who had sat in on my interview had requested a visit. Rachel was her name and she had sent me a letter. It didn't seem official; she had simply requested that I added her to my visitors' list. I had planned to discuss it with John, however, when he'd picked up the call, I could tell that he was busy. Just his tone told me, now was not convenient. I wasn't sure if he was at home or busy at work, but either way, he didn't have time.

"Did you call for a reason?"
"Um, no not really, it's just... I wanted to hear you. You know what it's like."
"Yes, well, sorry, Baby. Do you mind if I speak to you tomorrow? I'm really tied up at the moment. Are you sure you are ok?"
"Yes fine, it's nothing really."
"Ok, Baby, well, I'll speak to you tomorrow."

I didn't even get a chance to say goodbye, he'd ended the call. I had held the receiver in my hand before replacing it in the cradle. A single tear escaped down my cheek. I knew he meant nothing by it, but I just wanted to talk, to hear his voice and to see what I should do. On the outside, he'd always been my protector. In here I just felt so forgotten.

Josephine

I walked through the door of the Chambers with both purpose and apprehension. I wanted to know more of what had happened in Court Number Three. However, because of my immaturity and past experiences, I felt confused and unable to ask.

Robbie was at his desk and he was looking even worse than he had done the previous day. He was clearly hungover (again!) He appeared to have on a clean shirt and a different tie, but he was unshaven and his hair was all over the place. My mother would have been doing her pieces. One of her pet hates were untidy males. You would never have wanted to be unshaven in her presence. I think she considered it to be an actual sin. Ironic really, as almost every picture of Jesus had him sporting long hair and a beard! Mind you, the church is a completely different matter. Any sin in her eyes is immediately cleansed, and you are likely to get away with anything, so long you shove an Amen or Hail Mary into the mix!

Anyway, Robbie is sat with a coffee and a pile of case files, all bound with the now-familiar pink ribbon. He looks up at me.

"Are you Ok? Did you have a good day yesterday? I had half expected you back, you seemed so keen."
"Oh sorry, I wasn't feeling too good, so I went home. Do you know what happened?"
"In what case? Sorry, I lose track…. Ah yes, now I remember, they are back in today. They've got the clarity they needed over the forensics etc."
I think that I must have looked puzzled, as he immediately clarifies, "The stabbing of the young lad. We're representing the accused…. Remember? You made them coffee."
"Oh yes, no not that one… I meant, number three… The one that I went to in the afternoon."

"Um... I'm not entirely sure to be honest, I'm catching up with Maxine this afternoon, she's already over there. She's cross-examining, I think. Although, please don't quote me."

He shifts in his chair and then picks up a number of files. "Do you think you could sort out DX'ing these, please? Oh, and my coffee's cold, I could do with a refill."

I nodded my head, still wanting to know more about the case, but I was also aware that Robbie was busy. I didn't feel comfortable pestering him. I made my way into the kitchen to pour him his coffee as he'd requested, and also to make myself a milky tea. My palate wasn't sophisticated for coffee yet, and certainly not the tar that came out of the percolator which was perched on the side. If I ever did have coffee at home, it had to be Café Haag and made with lots and lots of warm milk.

I made my way back to Robbie, navigating around a number of Barristers, all busying themselves in the office. I could tell that I was in their way just by their body language. They were barking commands at various staff. One young girl, who was not much older than me was rushing about trying to find a file that was missing, that they had urgently needed for court.

I put the black coffee on the desk. "Robbie, sorry to bother you, but what is DX'ing? Is it filing or shredding? I'm not really sure." Smiling he laughs "Actually it's neither! I am so glad you asked… It's posting. See Jenny over there". He points to the young girl that I had seen rushing about. "When she's finished what she's doing, get her to help you."

Jenny was lovely and really helpful. She'd been working for the Chambers since she left school, and had been there for two years. She helped me send the files, and then we got chatting. I was asking about the cases and how the courts worked. She told me all about court listings, and how they told you what cases were on, and then she explained about the court results too. She said that they were published so you could easily find out the outcome to any case. That was all I wanted to know. I could easily find out what had happened without the need to bother anyone further.

Josephine

So, after four days of me making coffee, filing, DX'ing, and attending court, my work experience had come to an end. It had been interesting and had opened my eyes, but not really to the legal profession and its processes etc., but to how unfair, and how unjust life really was.

The murder case; although the accused had clearly done it, the barristers fought hard to have them acquitted. They tried their very best to discredit the victim, witnesses and the forensic evidence. It all seemed so wrong; it was just a game to them. It was all about them winning. They missed the point. An innocent life had been lost at these boys' hands, and they needed punishing. All they seemed concerned about was that no more lives should be disrupted, no more ambitions lost. But what if they needed to be disrupted, stopped? Ultimately prevented in carrying out any more horrendous acts? None of that mattered to them... so long as they won... And they did!! Only two out of the five were convicted, and only one for conspiring to murder. He was given 12 years! Yes, only 12 years! That is no time at all... And the other one... Well, he got a pathetic 3 years for violent disorder. It was all wrong. That young lad; their victim, he was lost. He no longer had his life. He no longer felt the sun on his face. Years later I discovered that the ringleader, the one who actually delivered the fatal blow; well, he'd been given unsupervised release for 3 days to attend a funeral, and wake. He absconded overseas; unpunished and ultimately free to do whatever he pleased. The law really was an ass.   And the paedophile case, that too was unjust. It was discontinued. The defence, (the smart-looking female barrister in her navy pinstripe suit) in her cross-examination of the victim, she had caused her to become so upset that she had clammed up. She'd been unable to say another word. They obviously had to adjourn the case, as the on-looking Judge said she clearly needed a break. But that was it. The End. She refused to go back in. She could not cope with the stress of it anymore, and therefore she took a permanent break from it. The victim, (a young girl) had been groomed by her teacher. He had used his authority to prey on her, in the very place that she should have felt safe. The system had let her down. And then again, in the very place that she was seeking justice, she was denied it. The system once again had failed her. She had sat there, tears rolling down her cheeks. She was the one who was made out to be immoral and not him! It was all wrong.

I didn't know how at the time, but I knew I wasn't going to let this go, I couldn't.

Josephine

Have you ever heard of the Near-Miss Syndrome? It's a theory that is usually used in relation to car drivers. For example, they nearly hit the car in front but they luckily don't. This is known as their near-miss. However, the theory describes that rather than check their speed and drive more carefully in future, they actually become more reckless. There are papers on it. Theorists Junko Shimazoe and Richard Burton, they document it. Although they call it the "justification shift." They first developed it in relation to the Space Challenger Accident, which took place in 1986... They determined that we actually think subconsciously (of course), that if it didn't happen last time, it wouldn't in the future. I remember listening to a journalist on the radio as he was explaining the theory some years later, and it made total sense to me. Just because something didn't happen this time, it didn't mean that the risks weren't there. In this scenario, the near-miss of getting a conviction filled the accused with a sense of arrogance, of victory and in turn they became even less careful.

Overtime, this syndrome and the "justification shift", it became very much my friend.

Superintendent Jo Gordon

It's funny really, I had never even dreamt about doing anything else. I had always wanted to be a Police Officer. I don't know what the pull was, but I can honestly say that when I first joined - young, keen and determined, I really wanted to make a difference. I wanted to help people.

Nowadays, however, it's not the desire to help that motivates me. Today it's all about self-preservation. I have given my all to this job, and every single one of those officers are my kids and I am the parent. Now as a parent, if I say NO to something, I expect my child (theoretically of course) to listen. What I don't expect is for them to go off behind my back, and start their very own little investigation!!

To say that I'm pissed off is an understatement. I am within touching distance of my next promotion, increased salary and pension…. I will not let her, nor anyone else get in the way of that. I've already sacrificed far too bloody much.

Shelley

I didn't really know why she'd come. You see, that DC, she came to visit me. Obviously, I'd been expecting her, as I'd put her on the visitors list, but I had only really done that out of curiosity. She was now a Detective Sergeant. She had got herself promoted. She came to sit opposite me and she asked me how I was. It was in my opinion a stupid question, as you could clearly tell how I was doing. Even I could see in the grainy stainless-steel mirrors that we have in here, that I look ill. I've aged and my skin looks grey. It's as if how I feel on the inside radiates on the outside, and I obviously don't say that in a self-complimentary, youthful and glowing sort of way! I'm broken and I look bloody awful!

She starts by saying that this is an informal visit, so I'm not under caution. She then goes on to ask how the appeal is getting on. This immediately confused me as surely, she doesn't want me appealing? Anyway, I told her that John was on the case and she'd need to talk to him about that.

She was writing notes as we were talking, but I'm not entirely sure on what. Then out of the blue, she asks me straight, that if it wasn't me who had killed Colin Joseph, did I have any idea who actually did? I just looked at her completely dumbfounded.

"Sorry, why are you here?" I felt my eyes narrow as I was suspicious of her motives... "I only agreed to having you here because I was curious as to why you had made contact... but you've not really told me anything of your motives... Look, do you know something that can help me? Or are you fitting me up for something else?"

"Look …. Sorry, I didn't mean to confuse you… but, I'm in a new department. Cold Cases and it's made me rethink your case. I'm just trying to get a better idea of the facts."

Instantly rage like a volcano has erupted from deep within my stomach... "THE FACTS?! It's a bit late don't you think?" I realise I'm shouting. She just stares over at me and says nothing. "I'm in this bloody place because of you! My kids are a mess, my mother will probably die before she sees me out of here, and you are telling me that you want to know the facts!!! ..... The fact is, is that I didn't bloody do it!" My mask had slipped but I didn't care. That's what this place does to you. I stood up abruptly. I had no intention of assaulting her but the guard, he rushes over anyway. He ends the visit, manhandling me (unnecessarily) and I am put back into my cell.

Josephine

I felt preoccupied and even Mum had noticed. I had felt such disgust and anger, since first sitting in that courtroom. There really was no justice.

I was in such shock initially after CJ had raped me. That alone would have been enough for anyone to deal with, but then I also had to manage the resulting pregnancy, and growing a baby without any support. Not even from Mum. It's hard when people think that you are a liar.

I completely understood, and I identified with that young girl. I knew exactly why she chose to give up with her court case, rather than get the justice that she so rightly deserved. It had turned into too much of a struggle.

When I had got home after the "accident." (Well... that's what Mum decided it was and I just couldn't be bothered to contradict her). I was too weak to go through it all again. I had never even considered tracing CJ and getting what?? An apology? Revenge? Justice? I knew he'd got an apprenticeship, but I didn't know for what company, and I had no clue what his actual name was. I did make some discreet enquiries at the Church, but no one seemed to know anything of his whereabouts, nor his full name. So, rather than go through the official channels, I too had given up... I decided it was better to let sleeping dogs lie.

Josephine

It was by pure fluke that I had made his acquaintance. I was running some errands for Mum in town, and I had decided to grab an iced finger from the bakery. As I stood in the queue idly daydreaming; a man was stood directly behind me. I found him a little close, but that wasn't why I turned around. The bakery walls were mirrored, and although his features were obscured because of the angles, I recognised him. I couldn't immediately place him, so I just smiled, assuming that he must have been one of Mum's church lot. He smiled back at me and we got chatting.

It was a day before my 17th birthday, but I still looked very much like a 14-year-old, especially as I wasn't one for wearing makeup. I also had on a summer dress which showed off my shapeless body. I had the physique of a boy. Small breasts, no curves; and I was to the onlooker, a child.

This man whom I thought was a friend was seemingly kind, and of no perceived threat to me. I had no qualms about buying my treat, and walking along to the park with him. We sat down on a vacant bench, and we continued chatting. It had only dawned on me once I had finished my snack, and I was still sat next to him, that I realised who he actually was. He was that monster, the one from Court Number Three.

Superintendent Jo Gordon

So, I've reviewed the files, and yes, she has identified a clear linked series, but I'm not convinced. I don't think that the "Body in the Wood" case is one of them. Similar MO granted, but not exactly the same. The other males were deceased over the past 30 odd years. Yes, they had been discovered in woodland, but all of them at the time had been reported missing and believed to have initially taken their own lives. It just wasn't enough.

John

I picked up the call and I could tell that it was official.

"Am I speaking to Mr John Jones?"

"Yes, who is this?" I answered uneasily...

"Um, I'm sorry to have to call you like this, but I'm phoning from the prison."

Instantly chilled, I know that something is wrong… and it seems forever before the female caller continues...

"Well, it's your wife. She has tried to hang herself."

I couldn't believe what she was telling me...

"Are you sure? Where? How?"

"I'm sorry, but the full circumstances need to be investigated, but it was this afternoon. She had had a visit from a police officer, and this seemed to have unsettled her. Then unfortunately, she found out that she was unsuccessful in the Family Day Ballot. It's our initial assumption that it was all too much for her…."

" Right OK, but…. How is she?" I say this hesitantly, I'm not sure I want to hear the answer...

"Well, she was taken to St Nicks and she's currently under sedation."

"What? Why?"

"I think it's to do with swelling on her brain and a lack of oxygen. They are trying to limit the damage."

Taking a deep breath. "Can I see her?"

"Yes of course…. Look, I know it's a lot to take in. Do you want me to text you the details of where she is? The ward, etc.?"

"Um yes, yes thank you."

"Ok I'll message you now, and then you'll have my mobile number, and if you need to ask or contact me over anything, don't hesitate."

"Ok thank you."

With that she has ended the call. I didn't even ask her name. I sit down at the kitchen table. My head in my hands. What the hell?

Superintendent Jo Gordon

"For goodness' sake! What were you thinking? Why in God's name did you visit her? I'd already said leave it with me, and what do YOU do? You stir up a flipping hornet's nest. Rachel!! She's on a bloody ventilator!"

DS Rachel Cooper just sits there on the other side of the desk. She says nothing. Just looks at me.

"So, I suppose you want me to fix this? Well, I'm not sure that I can!" *I say this dramatically*... "It's police contact! It will be a bloody IOPC referral! Look! …. Get out of my sight!"

With that, Rachel gets up and leaves the office. Her head hung. She doesn't even look at me, or try to explain her actions. I'm not even sure that she can.

Josephine

He had explained that he was new to the area. But unsurprisingly he had failed to mention the court case, or his near-miss!

I know it's not a great conversation starter… "Oh and by the way did I tell you I'm a….." Anyway, he was clearly moving on and I, it would seem was his next target. Unfortunately for him, and what he didn't know was he'd just made himself mine!

Superintendent Jo Gordon

So, I organised the drinks for the troops, and as I was feeling rather generous, I popped 250 quid behind the bar. I didn't do this to be kind. I just like to be the sort of boss that people cannot fathom. The harsh but fair, and not always predictable type. I have found that over the years, it keeps people on their toes. I also like the fact that if you're the one supplying the booze; tongues really do wag much more freely, and you find out what is really happening amongst your flock.

My chosen venue was "The Green Bottle". It was a backstreet boozer that was used to accommodating its regular police clientele. Back in the day, I think this is where the CID used to run most of their operations out of. How things have changed, no smoky offices to walk through, no station stamp on the arse of the new female officers! The job was unrecognisable from when

I had first joined, and in my opinion, some of those changes were not necessarily for the better.

I arrived a little later than most of them. I like to circulate without really being noticed. It helps you see who has allegiances. Who is clearly shagging whom, and it allows you to overhear conversations that would never be had back at the Station.

Anyway, I nip into the ladies and there are two officers chatting between cubicles.

".... She thinks there's something amiss, as apparently Ma'am was given something but nothing came of it. Do you remember? That night duty?"

"What night duty?"

"You know... That female? She had brought in a carrier bag and had given it to Josh. He'd taken it to Ma'am... she was flapping, telling him he had to arrest her... She had us searching by the Nick. Remember now? "

"Vaguely Hun."

"I still can't believe she hung herself!"
"Anyway, what's that got to do with it?"
"I dunno, but it seems off doesn't it?"
"Ok Miss Marple! Calm down with your conspiracy theories! God, I'm too pissed for this...."
(The chain pulls.)

Shit! I'm the chuffing talk of the Station! I didn't wait for them to come out. I couldn't... I rush through the door and I make my way through the crowd that I'd brought together. They were all merry and clearly enjoying themselves. I try to get past quickly but I'm stopped by some of B Team.

"Ma'am! Thank you so much. This was really kind." They all slur at me, heads nodding. I regain my composure and I try my best to hide my desperation to leave.
"Not at all, you have worked hard. You know, I like to give back." I say this hurriedly... I had tried not to make

any eye contact, but an old sweat, he was keen to have a chat. ...

"Ma'am, are you ok? You don't quite seem yourself...."

"Yes, I'm fine. I just realised that I had forgotten to do something. I've got to nip back to the office."

"Ah, ok... No rest for the wicked hey?!"

I don't reply as I think about what he's just said, and whilst stumbling towards the door, I try to make my escape.

I'd planned on standing up in front of the troops; asserting my authority and telling them to keep up the good work. I'd not drunk a drop of alcohol, but after what I had just heard, I felt incapacitated. Rather than rallying the troops, I'd discovered that they were all against me.

I then hear the creak of the ladies toilet door. I turn to try and find out who it was that was gossiping, but I can't see, and the harder that I try, the more difficult it gets.

I then hear my alarm clock... and I'm awake. My pyjamas are soaked in sweat, and I know that I need to sort this.

Superintendent Jo Gordon

I don't even shower. I get dressed and go straight in. Once I'm at the office, I immediately go to my desk drawer. Fumbling, I turn the key. Inside the drawer, sat the carrier bag that had been hand-delivered to me all those months ago. I reach in, grab out the knife, and the photo and in a moment of madness, and using a desk-wipe, I clean them. I cannot and will not have them casting any doubt on her conviction. I am not letting her ruin my career.

John

The girls were at school, so childcare wasn't an issue. I made my way straight over to the Hospital. She was in Sycamore Ward. After asking at the reception, they pointed me down the corridor to a private room. I could see a security guard stood just outside of the door. Through the slatted blinds, I could then make out her familiar form in the bed. There were tubes and monitors all around. I knew that she was my wife, but I didn't recognise her as the bubbly brunette, that I'd met on the train all those years ago. Although she was still alive. I knew that her soul had already left me.

Superintendent Jo Gordon

I had been busy and out at meetings all morning. I just found it on my desk. I looked at the letter. No stamp, no postmark. Did it get missed by the franking machine or hand-delivered? It was typed in caps, so there were no clues with the handwriting. The paper was standard issue white A4. I read out loud what it said...

WATCH OUT. I KNOW.

Without any hesitation, I screw it up and I put it straight into the bin. I don't know what it means and nor do I care. They can't touch me!

Josephine

Did I plan it? Well, I suppose I had a plan, so I must have. We met a few times, he seemed kind enough. He knew the exact right things to say to me. I could tell that if I'd been what I had seemed; a young naive child, I would have fallen for it. I would have been his prey.

He spoke nothing of his ex-wife and son, who was only a few years older than me. He'd reinvented himself and passed himself off as my protector. I was wise to it, however. I had been here before.

It was a late summer's afternoon. There was a denseness to the air, and he had persuaded me to go for a picnic. He had picked me up in town. I'd told Mum that I was volunteering again at the library. I had started there as something else to do, other than the church. Since what had happened, it always seemed so sour attending the cold stone building where my innocence was so brutally destroyed.

Anyway... Mum didn't mind me volunteering as she had always said... "Reading, Josephine is good for the soul". I couldn't be bothered telling her that I rarely read anything there, and that I just directed people to the correct departments; unpacked and displayed journals, newspapers, etc. I stamped their withdrawals, repatriated their returns. It was very process-driven, and I liked that. I also loved the smell. A pleasant musk always hung in the air. It was a mixture of dust, and the slow decaying of the paperbound books.

Anyway, he picked me up at the bus stop. He had a red hatchback, the type that I had learnt to drive in…. Yes, at barely 17 years of age, I had got my licence. I passed first time. I hadn't yet got a car for myself, but I just knew it would be a handy skill to have and I was right.

Off we go and I'm sat in the passenger seat. I have worn a dark blue dress. It was pretty but modest, with the hem just above the knee. He seems nervous, maybe a little edgy. He was busy telling me about these lovely woods where we were off to, when he places his hand on my knee and says... " I just want it to be special". At his touch, I try my hardest not to flinch. Since what had happened, I found that any close contact is more than a little uncomfortable. In fact, usually, I actively avoid it. Today, however, is different. Today I allow it. I endure it out of necessity.

He takes my brief, but noticeable recoil as nerves and so he pats my leg again. "It will be fine you know. I'll look after you." He's not overt in what he's got planned, but I know. He thinks that he is taking my virginity. A balding and quite disgusting 35-year-old male, thinks that he is about to experience my innocence. What he doesn't know however, is that another monster had already done that. I'm no more pure than I am a child, but that fact makes his intentions no less vile.

We arrive at the edge of a meadow. It's beautiful. Tall grasses sway in the light breeze, and there are a few remaining wild poppies and cornflowers clearly late in blooming.

He parks up and comes to my car door. Opening it for me, I step out. He really is trying to portray himself as very much the gentleman. We go to the boot of the car and he pulls out a carrier-bag. I can just about make out a pack of pork pies, sausage rolls, alongside some salted crisps, and a cheap-looking bottle of white wine. I gesture towards the bottle and he says..." To help you relax." He lifts out the bag and then rummages in the boot. "Damn it!" He says under his breath.
"What's the matter?" *I say this a little concerned, as he's clearly agitated.*
"Sorry darling, I've forgotten the picnic blanket."

"What's this then?" I say this whilst I am pulling at something blue.

"It's a tarpaulin…. but yes…. good idea. That will do nicely."

He pulls out the rolled-up sheet, and then he picks up the carrier bag of food and I begin to follow him. He helps me over the stile and into the meadow. I can hear the grasshoppers and I watch as a red admiral flutters ahead. It's such a beautiful scene. It would be the most romantic of places if we were young lovers, but we were not.

Josephine

It seemed like we had walked for miles. I could see that his hands were white, as the plastic from the bag had cut into his flesh.   It was hot and we were both perspiring. His shirt was beginning to stick to his back and my fringe had gone frizzy.

"Where are we going? I'm so tired... Are we nearly there yet?" As I said it, I didn't realise how childlike that phrase really was. It was like he was the Dad, and I his daughter.
He turned, smiling at me. "Nearly darling, we don't want to be disturbed now do we?"
I smile and nod as I try to keep my nerve. We eventually come to a wooded area at the edge of the longest meadow that I've ever seen.
"Here we are." He announces rather grandly...

He helps me over another stile and we are suddenly shaded. The sun is dappling through the trees and on to the dusty woodland floor. He pulls me close and I can feel his breath on my cheek. He nuzzles me. I try so hard not to be repulsed. Then he pulls away and I'm relieved.

"Right then! Are you hungry?" We devour the picnic, and I gulp down the first glass of white wine that he had poured for me… He immediately topped it back up…. "Thirsty, are we?" The crisps that he had selected had seemed especially salty and I was trying unsuccessfully to quench my thirst…

I start to feel more relaxed, and then I feel that his hand is creeping along my leg. He's moving up towards my inner thigh. "What are you doing?" *I say nervously.* "What do you mean? You know exactly what I'm doing, you naughty little girl."

He carries on despite my obvious jolt away. I can feel his hand moving further up. "NO STOP!" He doesn't stop and then I'm back with CJ and I can smell him.

My survival instinct, it has kicked in and before I know it, I've pulled a knife from my handbag, and rather cack-handily stabbed him in the back of his head. His eyes were instantly full of shock… and my instinct although initially it had made me fight, now I was definitely in flight. Without any hesitation, I get up and I run, boy do I run… I dare not to look back.

John

The Liaison Officer from the prison called me. She made all of the right sounds on the other end of the phone. She checked on my welfare and she was pleased to hear that I had been given some compassionate leave. Funny that! It's all people are these days; compassionate. They make all the right gestures and sounds, but they are empty, meaningless.

Since all of this has happened, I have not had a proper job. My firearms licence, it was taken away immediately after Shelley was charged. I think they, (Management that is) were scared that I'd "off" Jo! God, I hated her and probably would have done too, had I not needed to be there for my girls.

The Guvnor and Occupational Health gave me a home visit. I remember it well. They were sat in my lounge, and on my sofa, and giving me their sales pitch of how "the stress brought on by the circumstances means that we can't sign off on the risk assessment at present." No longer was the suspect the unknown risk; it was me. I was seen as the greater threat; a liability, and so, as they couldn't get rid of me, they found me a new role… "So, we have the perfect opportunity for you…. It's family friendly, and it will help you to develop in other areas…" Yup! They stuck me in a shit office job. Yes, the hours fitted around the girls, but I never joined to be a paper pusher. And now, after Shelley's suicide attempt, I was being given leave from that as well. Even pushing paper had become a too stressful a job for me!

The Liaison Officer, Jackie, wanted to let me know that they had formally transferred Shelley to a Secure Unit which was outside of the prison footprint. This was so that when she was well enough to be released from hospital, she would be cared for/ locked up there. "And with that in mind, I've gathered all of her personal effects together. Would you like to collect them or I can drop them off to you? I think you're on my way home."

She'd clearly decided that Shelley wasn't making it. It sounded like the call I'd had when my mother had passed away in the home. "Shall I box up her possessions?" I remember the Matron so well. My mother had had a stroke in her early sixties. They did their best for her at the home, but all that remained after her death were her scratched reading glasses, an old biscuit barrel, a few photos and her cat figurines. Tragic really.

"Um sorry, what exactly has she got there? I didn't think she really had anything personal as such."
"I'm not sure, but I know there's some correspondence, some toiletries maybe, and I seem to remember some sort of cuddly toy."

Of course, I think to myself. Mr Pickles! Maggie had insisted we send him into Mummy (her favourite toy) to look after her whilst she was away. I was petrified that first night when Maggie didn't have her comforting bunny; but my brave little girl…. she didn't even mention him.

Bless her, I remember when we had left him in Spain after a family holiday. That was a very different matter, and she had cried every single night up and until his FedEx return. But not this time, she wanted her Mummy to have some comfort. I well up thinking about the past, but then Jackie interrupts me... "So, shall I drop it off? Or will you have chance to come by?"

The thought of going back to the prison, it sent chills down my spine. I think back to when I was in CID, it was like my second home. I was always up there with my production orders, trying to get my clear-ups sorted...

Visiting Shelley there had really made me view the place from a very different perspective. I hated it there.

"Yes ok, thank you. Drop it off if you don't mind."
"Ok no bother. I'll pop by tonight."

With that, she was gone and I was back to the deafening silence and my thoughts.

Josephine

Sweat beads are cascading down my forehead and I can taste the salt in my mouth. I'm completely out of breath when I finally and gratefully see the car. I come to a stop by the stile and then I realise that I need to go back. If only to get my handbag and the car keys. I turn around and stumble back through the meadow. My head is fuzzy. I can't tell if it's still the effects of the wine or the shock. What the hell have I done? I reach the edge of the wood, and I make my way back to where I left him. I can make out his shape. I call out to him to see if I get any reaction. Nothing.

I move closer and I can clearly see that he is dead. He has glassy eyes and an awkward bodily position. I begin to panic. I can't see my bag. Then I see the strap. He must be lying on it. I go to move him, and with my first attempt being fruitless, (I had no idea just how heavy a dead body was) I try again and this time I manage to roll him sufficiently on to his side to slide my bag out. I look at him. He actually looks at peace.

I was still shocked at what I had done…. I knew that I had brought my dad's knife with me. But that really was just for my own protection. Not necessarily to kill him with. He may have been the teacher, but this time, it had been my turn to educate him. I just wanted to stop him and give that girl justice.

Catching sight of his watch on his wrist, I realise how late it is. Mother would be wondering where I was. That's the problem with the summer months, you never actually know how late it has got. I realise I've got to act fast, so I start by creating a pile of all the stuff that I need to take away with me. I place my handbag on one side, and then I collect up all of the picnic items and I stuff the wrappers back into the plastic bag. I would drop that into a bin on the way home. He unfortunately for me, wasn't going to be as easy a job to dispose of.

I needed a plan. I sat and thought for a while and then it came to me. I'd seen an article in one of the journals that I'd put out at the library. It wasn't the most inspiring of journal titles. "Journal for the Forensic Science " It was very technical, but I'd gleaned that the use of dental records and fingerprints, were routinely used to help identify an individual. I needed to make him unidentifiable…. I thought some more, and then I had my eureka moment. I would burn him!

I had already realised that he was too heavy to move by myself, and I had no one to help me. It wasn't like I could ask Mother to give me a hand. I'd asked her to help me when I was raped, and she didn't. She's definitely not going to help me cover up a murder!! So, taking a deep breath, I move to the side of him and I fish about in his trouser pocket. I can feel through the lining of the pocket that his body was still warm. A shiver creeps down my spine but I press on. I take out the contents; both his wallet and car key. The tarpaulin 'picnic blanket' had been a godsend as it was the perfect size for wrapping a body.

I was working quickly and I really hoped that he'd done his homework, and that this place was as remote as he had planned. I looked around and although there was not an abundance of cover on the woodland floor; the few stray sticks that there were, and any soil that I could scrape up, I used to cover the body with. Not so much to bury it, but to provide some sort of camouflage ahead of my return. My dress was dirty and wet-through with sweat. Surprisingly there hadn't been much blood, or any that there was had luckily soaked into his clothing. I left him concealed as best as I could, and I made my way back to the car. I ensured that I had picked up the carrier bag and my handbag, along with his keys and wallet. When I reached the stile to the left of the car, I stood on it. I strained to look back towards where I had just come from. I needed to be sure that nothing could be seen from the road. I didn't need anyone discovering him before I came back to complete the clean-up job.

Josephine

"Jesus, what happened to you? Are you ok?"

As soon as I'd put my key in the door, my mum had pounced on me. I had hoped that I could have got inside undetected, and at the very least washed my hands and face before she had started to interrogate me. I knew she'd want an explanation, so as I drove his car away, I came up with as plausible one as I could manage.

I drove near to home and I parked up. I made sure that the car wasn't overlooked by any houses, so I picked a spot at the edge of the local comp. It was the summer holidays; school was out, and the fields that surrounded it meant that I wouldn't be seen. I then walked the 15 minutes or so home.

My explanation to Mother was that the bus had broken down and that we (me and the other passengers) had tried to push the bus, and this had led to my rather dishevelled appearance. I also explained how it hadn't worked (pushing it, I mean...), so I had had to walk home anyway... and... that I had misjudged how long it would take me. I even added in the drama of being between bus stops when a replacement bus had sailed on past me! She seemed to buy it.

"Egg salad for tea? It's too hot to cook." She said... As I sat down, I noticed some old photos on the kitchen table.
"What are these Mum?"
"Just old pictures. Look at this one of you and your dad."
Mum looked at me, her eyes glistening. She must have been having a sentimental day.
"I remember that one being taken. Such happy days."

I turned it over. In Dad's handwriting it said 'Beachy Head 1976'.

Josephine

I barely slept. I knew I needed to be up early if my plan was going to work. I crept downstairs, not wanting to wake my mother. I didn't need a Spanish Inquisition, not now, and certainly not today.

I left her a note saying that I'd gone to visit Helen. Helen was an elderly parishioner who had recently moved to the coast. She was like a grandma to me and I'd visited her once before at her care home by the sea. It was a lovely place, beautiful views and a story that Mum wouldn't question, so long as I brought back a pack of extra strong mints. You see, every time I'd visit her when she lived down the road; you know, to pop in a casserole or cake that my mother had made. She would always and without fail, thrust a packet of mints into my hand. It was her way of saying thank you. Even last month when I popped down to see how she had settled in; she gave me the mints... Helen and her mints were the perfect alibi.

That morning I'd hurriedly eaten a bowl of cornflakes and had a strong cup of tea. I instantly regretted not leaving the cereal to soften a little longer in the milk, as I'd scratched my throat and I had a tickle of a cough. It was persistent and I desperately tried to stifle it ahead of leaving the house. I softly closed the front door and I was pleased that at least phase one had gone to plan. I hadn't disturbed my mother.

I walked the 15 minutes or so back to the car, and I was relieved that it was still there. I'd uncharacteristically been careless, and I had forgotten to lock it in my haste the previous evening. I chastised myself, but as no harm was done, I carried on with the plan. I drove to the nearest Esso and filled up. I also filled up the jerrycan that he had helpfully left in his boot. I was just about to drive off when thankfully, I remembered the mints! Running back in and putting them on the counter, the young lad at the till didn't even look up. He just grunted as I placed the exact change in front of him. I had done the same with the petrol, I mean by providing the exact amount owed…. My dad when he was alive, he used to get me to fill up and it was always my mission to fill up to the decimal. Although, in those days the attendant would let you off the odd pence, but Dad would have none of it. He liked the skill and the precision of it. He'd definitely passed his meticulous ways on to me. God, how I missed him.

Driving away from the petrol station, I felt pretty reassured that the lad wouldn't have been able to describe me. I was in and out just like a ghost. I laughed to myself. Even after my small stint in a courtroom; I often ran an internal dialogue of what a barrister might say in my head. "So, you can't recognise the defendant, but you do remember that she bought extra strong mints? Do you know how ridiculous that sounds?... Did she intend to kill him with her minty fresh breath?!!" Keeping myself amused, I ran a number of different, and outrageously stupid scenarios, and then in no time at all I had arrived back at the lane.

I park up. However, rather than unpack everything straight away, I think it would be prudent to check if he were still there. At this point I wished I'd borrowed the neighbour's dog, as I could have pretended that I was out giving him his daily exercise, had the place been awash with police.

I climbed over the first stile and into the meadow. I then stomped my way over to the next, and the woodland beyond. In my mind's eye, retracing my steps. I got to where I thought he should be but he wasn't. No mound, no tarpaulin, no nothing!

My mouth goes immediately dry as I start scanning the woodland floor for him. I didn't camouflage him that well. I didn't have the time, nor the raw materials. Autumn had yet to come, so no fallen branches or rusty coloured leaves to have aided me. I felt my breakfast rising into my mouth and it smarted my scratched throat as I uncontrollably throw up. The realisation hits me that he must still be alive. I am in real danger. I turn immediately and run back to the car. I need to get out of here and fast.

Josephine

My whole body is full of adrenaline as I make it back to the lane. I get straight into his car and speed away. My foot is pressed firmly to the floor. Then as I look ahead, I feel like I'm having a moment of deja vu. In front of me on the bend of the lane is a stile. It looks exactly the same as the one that I had just vaulted over, and in a moment of clarity, I think... Maybe I stopped too soon?

Taking a deep breath and hopeful, I park up again.

I climb over the stile, run through the meadow, over the second stile, and there ahead of me I can just about make out a mound on the woodland floor. Tears of joy escape from my eyes at the realisation that his dead body still remains. After a brief moment of celebration, I finally compose myself, and I get to work.

John

It had been a really busy week. Both of the girls had their end of term shows, and considering what had been happening in their little worlds of late, they absolutely smashed it. I was so proud. Shelley's mum and dad came to watch them as well, and to make it more of an occasion, we had also taken them out for a pizza tea. Obviously, their mummy was missing, but it almost felt like normality. They still didn't know and nor would they ever know why Mummy was in hospital. They just knew that the very clever Doctors and Nurses were making her better again. How I hoped and prayed that were true.

***

We returned late from the meal and in the porch was a brown cardboard box. It blocked the entrance to the front door, so I picked it up and brought it in with me.

In a rush to get the girls into bed, and having popped it on the kitchen side, I thought no more of it. It was a week or so later when I noticed it again and I had a look at its contents. Inside was Mr Pickles, Shelley's cocoa-butter moisturiser, and some letters. I opened the cocoa-butter and squeezed a little out into my hand. I took a deep breath. I'd not smelt her for so long and instantly the chocolatey fragrance catapulted me back to much happier days. Her svelte figure wrapped in a towel after a shower and her lathering herself in this heavenly stuff. God, I missed her. All of her, her laugh, her touch. Just knowing that she was sat in the same room, it was enough for me. We didn't even have to talk. She completed me.

I then turned my attention to the letters and this one in particular, caught my eye. The address on the envelope was in handwriting that I'd seen before. It was marked confidential but I was pretty sure that Shelley wouldn't mind if I opened it up. It would have already been opened by the prison staff anyway. I read the first couple of lines and my mouth became immediately parched. Why the hell didn't she tell me?

Josephine

What is it with the English weather? One day scorching hot and the next, cold and drizzling? Well... today we had rain. We'd endured the heatwave for weeks, but today it had finally broken. It was wet but I wasn't moaning; it was a welcomed break and it allowed me to get on with things in a little more comfort.

Once I had calmed down over the initial fear that he might still be alive, or had even been discovered, I set to work ... I wasn't sure really which would have been more of a disaster for me... him chasing me or the cops... but as neither right now were of my concern, I put these thoughts to the back of my mind as I got on with my task.

In his car he kept a set of tools; in particular a shovel and a small axe... Both of them came in very handy. I carried the items over to the wooded area, and towards his body which was still wrapped and partially hidden on the pebbled and dusty floor. I felt uneasy as there was a definite chill to the air.

Anyway, I brushed off the sticks and loose dirt, and I unwrapped the tarpaulin. His eyes were vacantly looking up at me, and I was shocked that his body was so solid to the touch. Almost fixed in position. I knew I needed to make his body unidentifiable, but I quickly realised that the removal of his teeth was going to be tricky. His jaw was shut tight. I decided that chopping off his fingertips would be much easier, so I began searching in his tool bag and I came across a pair of bolt cutters. They were made for the job, and after only a few practice-goes, I'd perfected my technique. Carefully snipping, I removed each one of his fingertips and toes. I laid them to one side, making sure that I counted to ten, twice. I couldn't risk leaving anything behind.

I then went back to his jaw. I was hoping the rigor mortis would have started to subside but it was still clenched. There was no other way, so grabbing the axe and lifting it high over his head, I smashed it directly into his face. It was a messy job, but it had the desired effect of loosening most of his teeth. My biology lessons with Miss Herbert were finally of use, as I meticulously counted out 32, (the number of teeth that a grown adult has.)

John

It was the breakthrough that we needed. It was the new evidence. Well, it would have been had the Enc. part still been present in the envelope. The handwriting I'd still yet to place, so I was unsure of the author, but I was pretty sure that this was a confession. I read and re-read the scrap of paper that the envelope contained.

My Darling Michelle,

I'm so, so sorry.

Words cannot express the remorse at the damage that I have caused. I never meant to get you mixed up in this. All I wanted to do was protect you. The enclosed explains everything. I have already passed a copy to the police. Soon my darling, this nightmare will be over, I promise. Stay strong.

Love M x

Enc.

The words jumped off the page;

SORRY,

MIXED UP,

PROTECT YOU,

ENCLOSED.

I went through the other letters but there was nothing of significance. There were a couple of photos and cards that the girls had sent in, but nothing of what I sought. I picked up the box to make sure, tipping it upside down but I came up empty-handed. I needed to know what all of this meant. I had a few obvious leads but the author was for now, a mystery ... and the recipient unfortunately was still in a coma. I was desperate, so although not ideal, but without hesitation, I called Jo.

Josephine

So, I'd done it. I had disposed of his carcass. I could still feel the heat of the flames against my scorched skin. I had had no idea just how instantly the flames would take hold. I left the scene of my crime as soon as I could. I was worried that the smoke and flames might catch the attention of a passer-by. I'd already dug a shallow grave. It was difficult in the parched soil, but I had managed to roll him over into it. I was hoping that any remains after the fire would settle into the soil and be hidden.

All of this was new to me. I had a loose plan, but it was definitely organic in its evolution. Having done the hard part, I was now driving down the motorway. The weather hadn't improved, and the summer drizzle was hanging about, so the wipers were having to work hard at keeping the road visible. The radio was blaring and I was listening to Prince's 'When Doves Cry'. Fate it would seem had a hand in all of this, as ironically years later, I had discovered that doves symbolise a release of hate and revenge in your heart. This whole recent experience had definitely been cathartic for me.

It was late morning and I had reached my destination. It had taken me over 2 hours. The final part of my plan, I felt was an absolute stroke of genius. This I hoped would provide a kind of justice and finally give closure to his victim.

John

I rang her mobile and waited for her to pick up but she didn't. After just a few rings the phone went straight to answerphone. This was very unusual, she rarely let this happen. If she was in a meeting, she'd duck out to answer it. If she were in an interview, she'd leave her phone with her latest protégé to act as secretary. If she could have had it surgically attached, I think she would have done so. This was definitely out of character for her. Jo never worried about calling me. In fact, at one point just after the trial, she'd become a bit of a nuisance. I wasn't sure if her recent need to keep in touch was to gloat about Shelley's conviction or to try and rescue some of our past relationship. God, she was so deluded. She was so used to getting what she wanted and she had never really got over us. I knew this by the way she always made a point of seeking me out. I initially thought that's why she'd befriended Shelley to get to me. I couldn't believe the fact that I was off her radar long enough, for her not to have realised that I'd got married and had a couple of kids!

Anyway, I knew something was wrong, it had to be. I tried once more, however, this time it went straight to voicemail, no pre-rings. Had she switched it off? This was a concern as I was desperate to know what she knew. What was she covering up this time?

Superintendent Jo Gordon

Shit, John is ringing me. What the hell does he want? Was it him who sent me that note? I press the call-reject button and I let it go to answerphone. I can't deal with any questions right now. I need time to formulate a plan and an interruption is not going to help me think.

Josephine

I never really set out to do what I did. It all just fell into place. It was fate. Well, that's what I told myself. The realisation that there were more like him spurred me on. I know it's not HIM but I didn't see why that mattered. I could still make a difference. I could still stop them.

So, the first time was easy. I say easy, but what I actually mean is that it all went to plan. I had gotten rid of the body and any forensic evidence. Of which I had later found out that I had managed to achieve this more by fluke than through design. Yes, I'd done some research but nothing that granted me the protection that fate had. It didn't want me to be found out. It knew that I was here to do a job.

I dumped the car after my long motorway journey at the Beachy Head Bottom car park. That photo that my mum had found the day before, had been the most perfect of timings. It provided me with the final piece of my plan. I left his car unlocked and I made sure that his wallet and keys were left inside. I had already disposed of the axe, cutters, and shovel on route. Handily, I had spotted a skip at the side of the road. I had hurled them in. They were burned anyway so they were not much use to anyone. I still remember the heat of that fire; it had caught me a bit by surprise. Anyhow, it all worked in my favour as any evidence was immediately destroyed.

After dumping the car and retrieving the mints, I caught the train back up to London, and I made my way home. Mum was none the wiser. I'd managed to sneak upstairs before she saw me and I had showered myself quickly. I came down already dressed for bed and in my pyjamas. It wasn't so unusual for me to do this. I just explained it away as being a busy day of travelling. Mum had already spied the mints, so after checking that

Helen was ok, she didn't quiz me any further. If only she really knew what I'd done with my day. I felt in control, elated. Now all I needed to do was keep an eye on the papers and hope that nothing came back to me.

Josephine

For months and months, I waited and nothing... No breaking news of "Burned Remains Discovered". Nothing of "Acquitted Paedophile Presumed Dead!" .... and then in the Dentist waiting room ahead of my yearly check-up, I see it. In Chat Magazine, as clear as day... I would never have thought it to have ANY newsworthy content. But there it was, an article by the victim's sister. She was clearly cashing in, but in black and white I see the headline of... "Sister Gains Closure After Horrific Abuse!" I was absolutely jubilant! So much so, that my mood had lifted from the dread that I had felt at being at the dentist, and I practically skipped into the treatment room for my polish and scale.

I knew that the article wasn't directly from the victim, but I'm sure much of what was reported was true. I felt happy that I'd helped her. My act had certainly helped me. It was therapy and that's what I told myself when I identified monster number two.

John

My life had shifted so dramatically and I don't really know how I kept going. Shelley's mum helped out as much as she could, but I really felt like I was drowning. I'd tried Jo a few times and left a couple of voicemails. I'm sure she must know something.

Life had become overwhelming of late; I was constantly firefighting and I never knew which blaze I should tackle first. I was pulled in all directions. The appeal, the girls, work... Shelley…. and even visiting her had become a chore. She was hooked up to various machines, and she didn't even know I was there. I almost felt like it was a waste of my time… I could also see that the girls just weren't happy. Friendships were strained and they were no longer being invited for playdates. Also, every morning one or other of them had a tummy-ache ahead of school. I'd kept them as sheltered as I could, but of course, all of this had still impacted on them massively.

I tried my best to be both a Mummy and a Daddy to them, but I don't think I was overly successful at either role. Everything was just so hard as I was permanently and inevitably preoccupied elsewhere.

I had gone back to work but I wasn't really in the game. I was on reduced hours on advice from Occupational Health and I was grateful, but how had it come to this? I WAS a highflier. I had a lovely home, a beautiful wife, happy and loving kids. I was excelling in my career and I had been the youngest SFO (Senior Firearms Officer) on the team. I'd been promised big things, and yes, I'd coasted for a bit when the girls were first born, but that's normal for any new parent... sleepless nights and all. I had a plan, a goal and now look at me. Sat at a desk, I had become what I had despised. I was essentially the 'station cat'.

Josephine

So, after being a Volunteer at the Library for what seemed like forever, I was eventually offered a paid position. The timing was perfect as I'd just left school, having completed my A-levels. I had had no aspirations to go to university as I didn't really see the point. After all, what did you really end up with? A lot of debt and it only delayed you in starting at the bottom again. It's not as if Mum would have supported me anyway. I mean that both emotionally and financially. Her viewpoint was; "Well, I never went and it never did me any harm". I have a feeling that if Dad were still alive, I would have gone. He'd have steered me towards it. He always wanted the best for me and that would have meant a university education. My, how things had changed since his death. I doubt he'd even recognise his little girl. On the outside I was still a vulnerable looking child but, on the inside, I was anything but. My education was from life's hard knocks and I was embracing my mother's mindset. I didn't need a university degree; I was doing just fine on my own.

Superintendent Jo Gordon

Thankfully, I've not received any more of those notes, and John he has finally stopped calling me. I feel that things are levelling up. The investigation into DS Rachel Cooper's conduct has found no wrong-doing on the part of the police. I was grateful that she had at least declared her visit as not official; so, we, I mean she, was in the clear with the IOPC (Independent Office of Police Complaints).

I have also heard through the grapevine that Shelley has been moved to a rehab centre. It beats prison I suppose, although I am not aware of her progress or whether she is even conscious. To be honest I've lost interest now. I did this as soon as there were no issues over our conduct. I have begun to distance myself as far as possible away from John, Shelley, and DS Cooper. I need to keep myself out of it. Mud sticks you know!

Lately, I have also shifted my focus back on the troops and our borough objectives. I've not had any praise from the top recently, and I need to rectify this. Time to shine!

Josephine

I got fully settled in at the Library as a paid employee. My shifts varied depending on demand. The school holidays were our busiest time as we catered for the increased footfall. This obviously led to a reduction in the amount of time that I had available for my other pursuits.

I'd taken to checking on which type of cases were running, before I wasted any of my valuable time venturing out to this court or that. This allowed me to be more efficient and focused in my approach. I'd bob in and out to get a feel of the case and I always did my best to blend in. Be part of the furniture. I was a silent and hopefully unnoticed observer. Back when I originally began my quest, there were fewer cases being brought to trial. The ones that were, focused on the immoral religious workers, priests and the like, and on the staff who worked at the childrens homes; the type that HE had been brought up in. These people were the lowest of the low. They had used their position of trust to exploit their young and very vulnerable victims. There were very few disguised within the family unit. Then one day I came across an abusive stepfather. He had been welcomed into the family home, only to exploit this new family that he had vowed to his wife to care for and protect. I saw the listing and although I knew it had started the previous Monday, I hoped that by the Wednesday, (my day off) it was still in progress.

It was often the case that when it got all too much for the defendant; their underlying guilt meant that they changed their plea. Those cases I didn't mind. Those defendants acknowledged their crime and took their punishment. In those cases, the court was usually adjourned and only reconvened for sentencing. I had absolutely no interest in cases where justice was served. The system had worked. They did not need my assistance. The only downside, of course, was the unfortunate waste of my time having sat in on it in the first place.

Josephine

The Wednesday morning had arrived. I put on a black trouser suit and quickly made myself presentable before getting into the car and driving over the bridge to the Crown Court. This court was nothing like the Old Bailey. It was a modern 1960's concrete creation. A horrible looking building, but it was the perfect stage for the many horrendous crimes that were retold within those walls.

This particular case told of a predatory stepfather who had made himself so indispensable to his victim's mother, that she turned a blind eye. She had ignored the years of unthinkable acts, that he had inflicted on her then six-year-old daughter.   She made a choice; financial security over her own flesh and blood. It was the very worst type of neglect.

The victim who was now 17 had confided in her teacher at school. Mrs Graham had seen academic talent in her pupil, but couldn't fathom why she wasn't performing. She had taken the necessary time out to listen to this troubled teen and in doing so, she had opened up Pandora's box.

Unfortunately, although supported by the lovely Mrs Graham, the victim's day in court did not result in the justice that you would have expected. No, the day that I sat in the public gallery, I didn't hear how her (the victim's) childhood was snatched away at the hands of a controlling monster. No, I heard the mother cruelly testifying against her own daughter. Words such as fantasist, jealous, slanderer were being bandied about by her and were echoed by the Defence Barrister. Her own mother branded her a liar. She told the court that her daughter had been jealous of the love and affection that the defendant (her husband) had shown her. They painted the victim as troubled and unreliable.

Unfortunately, and also miserably for the victim that was all the jury focused on. So, when I heard the court result a week later and I discovered that he'd been acquitted, my blood was boiling. I knew I had to give her justice. Unfortunately, I also knew that I looked nothing like a six-year-old. I had to do something, but I needed a plan.

Josephine

You would not believe how easy it is to track people down. Telephone directories, voters' registers, newspaper articles, Companies House, etc. Each of these publications give you a clue as to where a person resides. In the case of the "Stepfather", he was very easy to trace... I hadn't needed to use any of the resources from the library. He was a plumber, and after a quick search in the Yellow Pages, I had the home address of where he and his bitch of a wife lived.

All I needed to do now was to instigate a chance meeting, and for me to act young and vulnerable enough to attract this pervert's attention.

Josephine

It took some time but I'd finally worked it out. I had a plan. I started to watch his house. In fact, the first time that I saw him I thought I'd got the wrong address. He looked nothing like the upstanding male that I'd seen in the courtroom. He had looked every bit of the 'respectable breadwinner and father', as he stood in the dock in his clearly expensive and well-fitting suit. No wonder the jury had got it so wrong. Now however, he was more akin to a ferret. In fact, that was the nickname that I gave to him. He was a horribly skinny male. He had beady little eyes with a shock of blond hair. He looked really scruffy in his t-shirt and jeans combo. Every morning he was up early and so was I. From afar, and in my little Fiat Panda, I'd watch where he went. It was clear he was still working, so his business hadn't been impacted by the court case.

Anyway, today was the day. I decided I needed to make contact. Obviously, having just turned 19, there was absolutely no way I'd pass for a prepubescent, but I could definitely pass as a naive schoolgirl who sadly had just been dumped. I had already been to the local outfitters and purchased the local Grammar's rather distinctive uniform of a kilt, shirt, and blazer. Handing over the money to the shop assistant, I wished I'd decided upon the local Comprehensive School as my cover. The uniform would have been a quarter of the price. Sadly, the wage of a Library Assistant wasn't much, and this had practically taken my whole month's money. It was good that I had savings, otherwise, Mother would have had something to say when I didn't furnish her with my month's rent.

I had already tracked him down to a semi-detached, literally around the corner to where he lived. He had been in and out all day. Back and forth to the van. I needed to time this right. I parked up around the corner and I fashioned my hair into a messy bun and I made myself look as young as I possibly could. Nervously, I walked up towards the address but then I realised that the van had gone. In all my preparations, I'd only gone and missed him leaving. Scolding myself at the lost opportunity, I started heading back to my car. Then I heard it. The rattle of a transit van coming along the street. It was him! He'd obviously forgotten something and needed to return. Fate once more was on my side. I just knew it!!

Taking a deep breath, I knew it was now or never. I ran back towards the address. Timing was everything and I had to get this right. He left his van and went back into the address. I could see movement through the high hedge to the left of me, and I hoped that he was about to come back out to the street. I made my play and bingo, our paths crossed! Him walking into me and me rather dramatically falling to the floor. My backpack with my books also spilling out onto the path.

"Oh, sorry love, I didn't see you there."

"It's OK. It's my fault." *Making my voice sound as weak and as small as I could.* I looked down at the floor, trying desperately to look embarrassed by the situation. I began to scrabble about picking up my spilled property from the pavement. Ferret bent down and he picked up one of my exercise books, clearly noting the name that I'd written on the front. He then reached out a fingernail bitten hand to help me up.

"Come on then Lizzy. Let's get you up."

He looked down at my knee and spotted that I had ripped my tights.

"Blimey, I really knocked you flying. Are you ok?"

I nodded my head making sure that I avoided any eye contact. I knew I had to play this just right.

"Look sorry…. Do you want me to drop you somewhere?"

Looking up at him, I gave a coy smile and he smiled back. "Um…. Do you mind?" I had some loose hair that was cascading at the side of my face. I twirled my finger briefly in it. I'd seen it on the TV and I would have tried anything to gain his interest in me.

"No, not at all, it will be my pleasure. Where are we off to?"

"Not far... Just around the corner...." Pleased with myself I got into his van. There was quite a lot of rubbish, so I shifted slightly to get some legroom in the crowded footwell. As I did so, I showed some of my thigh which was under my kilt. Ferret clearly enjoyed this sight, as I caught him looking at me out of the side of his left eye. He reminded me of a crocodile due to his sideward glance and by the way that he was smiling. I let him drop me at the nearby estate. I needed somewhere that meant he didn't actually get to know my address. "Just here. Thank you."

"Okey Dokey Lizzy." He pulled over and I got out closing the van door behind me.

"You take care now." He shouted this with a wide grin through the van's open window. I watched him drive off, away from the estate before I made my way back to my car. I wasn't sure if it had worked, but I'd definitely made his acquaintance.

John

So, I got the call. It was the Hospital where Shelley was. I took a deep breath so I was ready for what the male-sounding voice was about to tell me. I was prepared for the worst. Tears, instantly filled my eyes when he said the words "Your wife, she's awake!" I could not believe it. They had written her off, oh my goodness, even I had written her off! I didn't even ask him anything further of her condition, telling him simply and urgently "I'm on my way!"

I immediately logged off of the computer. "She's awake!" I shouted this as I ran out of the office and towards the car park.

Superintendent Jo Gordon

Things have definitely settled down. I took the troops out for their 'well done' piss up and I thoroughly enjoyed it too. I was back to feeling on top. I even took home a little prize. A young probationer. Totally unethical I know, but he enjoyed it as much as I did. Cougar? Is that what I am? Haha, I've still got it!

Rachel has also finally stopped going on about that bloody linked series. Even if there is a link between the other cases, it's irrelevant. I know Shelley did it. Gerald said that she was definitely hiding something and I'm inclined to agree with him. After all, he is the expert in psychology, and I am the expert in the law. I can tell a wrong-un immediately.

My little chat with Kevin has clearly worked too, as he's definitely been managing Rachel. She's no longer the loose cannon that I'd begun to worry about.

Josephine

For months I kept bumping into him and on our latest encounter, I made up a sob-story that my boyfriend had just dumped me, saying that I was ugly. He, on hearing this immediately sensed his in, and he told me just how beautiful I was. He also told me that he would be proud to have me as his girlfriend.

It was textbook; He did what all good groomers do. They play on their victim's insecurities; If the girl is told she's fat, they say she's thin. Ugly and she's beautiful. They make them feel special, earning their trust, and then boom! They are not a predator; they are the protector and as such, they can do absolutely anything - or so old Ferret Face had clearly thought!

We made a plan to meet. I'd hinted that I was a virgin and I could almost see the drool on his lip. He really made my skin crawl, but I knew I had to carry on. He had to pay. He had not learnt his lesson from his spell in court. No, his near-miss had taught him absolutely nothing. He clearly felt untouchable.

It was late spring, so the evenings were beginning to get longer. He had picked me up at the corner of the Estate and we were on our way out to the country for a late afternoon stroll. My idea of course. I had said that it would be nice to be somewhere where no one knew us, or would notice if we held hands or …. anything else. I got into his van. I was wearing a short summer dress and I was a little cold; so, although flat-chested, my nipples were proud and clearly visible under the thin material. I had my hair tied up, but I hadn't put any make-up on. I had made some effort, but I still wanted to look every bit a schoolgirl. He had made an effort too. He smelt clean and wore after-shave. It perfumed the van and it had managed to pleasantly disguise its usual stink.

I had already scoped out the area. The Ordnance Survey Map, which once I had considered my enemy, was now a friend. I was now so grateful to my dad, for all of the time that he had spent with me over my long summer holidays. Our coast-to-coast walks and my resultant navigation skills meant that I was a very proficient map-reader. I even reminisced over the previously hated times when we had been soaked through due to the poor weather, and I had suffered from painfully blistered feet. Now, however, all of that had seemed so worthwhile as I had easily been able to identify the perfect woodland spot for my tried and tested plan. I knew I was in a different county but the same principles applied. Location, location, location.

We parked up at the edge of the dense tree-covered area. I slid out of the van as he walked around to meet me. Hardly containing himself, he walked towards me, backing me up against a wooden post and rail fence. I felt the wood painfully hit my spine.

"No! Not here! Someone might see."

"Ok then, where? Oh god, I've been waiting for this."

Me too, I darkly thought.......

We walked holding hands. His pace was purposeful. His impatience, clearly evident. We arrived deeper in the woods and I finally let him kiss me. Eagerly he grabbed at me, pushing me backwards towards the trees. I was pinned, trapped against an old oak tree. I then felt him bend down and try to remove my knickers. He was still kissing me and as he did so, he was grunting and sounding just like a snuffling pig. It was all moving much quicker than I had anticipated and I couldn't let it happen, not again... I then heard the zip of his fly being undone…. My heart was racing and I knew that it was now or never. I had to act. I reached into my bag which was slung across my body and then holding firmly on to my dad's knife, I pulled it from my bag and I plunged it purposefully into his neck. It connected just above his shoulder-blades. He had no time to react. The shock took hold and he suddenly dropped to the floor. I had done it again! I stepped over him and I think there was a short moment of him snatching his last breath but I couldn't really be sure. Anyway, I felt nothing but exhilaration!

Number two, done!

***

Time as it always did, was escaping from me. That was the problem. My mum always wanted to know where I was and what time I'd be home. She had to control everything. I was a loner, so I had no friends. Often, I had to invent work gatherings just to give me the freedom so that I may follow my destiny. Looking at my watch I knew that tonight, all that I had the time to do was to cover over the body, and hope that no one found him before I had enacted my more permanent solution.

Tomorrow, thankfully was another day

John

When I got there, she was sat up in bed. She was still very confused and I could tell that she was having difficulty in recognising me. Her voice was raspy, but I think this was more due to the fact that she had not spoken in months, rather than any lasting effects of what she'd done to herself. I had so much I wanted to ask her. "Why?" being the most pressing of my questions. I didn't want to tire or stress her, however, so I stayed off that subject. I just asked her how she was feeling and I gave her a few sips of water.

I started telling her about Maggie and Heidi but I could see the exhaustion, confusion, or both start to creep across her face, and so I decided not to talk at her anymore, and to leave it there for the day. I was just so happy that she was awake. I knew this was just the beginning and that it would be hard, but I had a positive feeling that I was going to get my Shelley back.

Josephine

I walk in the door a little later than my usual 7 pm. Mum instantly looks me up and down. "Where did you get that from? A bit tarty for the library isn't it?" Her harsh Irish accent accentuates the word "tarty". I'm still in my summer dress, and by some fluke, it still looks clean and in no way associated to the brutal murder that it's just been an accomplice to. Its very presence had sealed the deal in making Ferret Face take the bait.
"Um, I bought it, Mum. A new shop in town. I didn't wear it to the library. I changed into it afterwards."
"For what purpose? In fact, where have you been?"
Her strong accent continuing to emphasise her disgust.
"Just out with some friends."
"Looking like that? Well, Josephine, I don't want to hear about you getting into trouble again. You know what happened the last time." Her words are barbed. She doesn't say it out loud but I know what she's talking about. She still thinks the pregnancy was my fault. She

never speaks of it and neither do I. It's our dirty little secret.

"Anyway, wash up, dinner is in five minutes. Come on young lady, quick, quick!"

You would think that I was a silly, young slip of a girl and not the strong and independent woman who had single-handedly now rid the world of two monsters, and was readily prepared to cleanse the world of more. I nodded my head and I took the stairs up to the bathroom where I scrubbed my hands and face clean of him. I then made my way back down the stairs and into the kitchen where I then tucked into a steaming ale pie. I was absolutely famished.

Central Station Female Locker Room

(It's empty except two chatting female officers).

"You did what?"

"Yes, I sent her a letter, I just popped it on her desk."

"Bloody hell, why? Are you mad?"

"No, I'm not. She swans around acting as if she owns the place."

"You do know how bleeding ridiculous that sounds? Of course, she owns the place! She's the Gaffer!"

"Not of me, she's not, and certainly not of Nick. He was shit faced and she took him home. He didn't know what he was doing? She bloody well did. She just takes. It's an abuse of position or something.... "

"Yeah, or something. So, what did the letter say?"

"Well, nothing really, I left it a bit cryptic but I wanted her to stop and think for a bit. She messes up people's lives. I loved him and she's destroyed it all."

"This sounds like a bloody domestic... We'd be nicking the ex - YOU - for mal coms if this were a call."

"Yeah, I know, I was so angry though... And did you see her at the drinks the other night?"

"No not really I was a bit busy myself..."

*"Yeah, and I really don't get what you see in him. He's a big dick. You do know that?" (*colouring up the other officer says with a smile.)

"God, I hope so!"

" Ah stop it you perve'. You're worse than the lads. Anyway, she took that Joel home, and I'm sure his Mrs is having a baby."

*"657 receiving" (*the officer's radio interrupts the girls gossiping.)

"Shit! I gotta go, Hun, that's my Skipper."

"Yeah, go ahead Sarge. " (answering the radio.)

"Where the chuff are ya? We've been waiting in the carrier for the last ten minutes, get your arse out here now."

"Coming Sarge, sorry I got tied up."

Josephine

My mum didn't know that I had taken holiday from work, so I was up early and left as if I were off to the library. My preparation of having my car parked on the other side of the woods, ahead of our arrival yesterday was genius. It made the plan run smoothly, as I had had no issues getting to and from the area. There was no need for me to use public transport, or to be spotted walking along the lanes. I needed to be like a ghost. In and out, and leaving absolutely no trace.

I was ready, I was rehearsed, and I was so calm this time. I knew exactly what I was doing. I got straight to work. Once I'd finished the prep work, I made sure that I picked up his keys and wallet (and the bits I'd removed). I had worked quickly and I was soon due to leave, having one last check that the body was burning well. Happy that it was, I made my way over to his van.

I had some concerns that his death, might not be as believable as the last one. You know, that he'd topped himself. The main issue was that his wife had publicly supported him. Would she buy the fact that he'd done this? It was a risk but I couldn't think of another way of explaining his permanent disappearance, well not without a body. Putting it to the back of my mind, I carried on with my plan and I drove the three hours to the coast. I hoped that the police would find the van unlocked with his personal possessions, and just put two and two together.

I was just setting the scene and about to leave the van in the clifftop car park when I spotted a note in the front of the windscreen. It clearly said *SORRY!* Underneath it continued. *No change, gone to get some. Be back in five minutes.* This was perfect. It said *SORRY!* I presumed it was his writing as I'd never seen anyone else use the van. There were no apprentices or the like, so I carefully ripped off the bottom half of the note and left the top bit with his wallet. That note had been a gift from God!

Then as I was leaving on foot and walking away, a grey estate car drove into the car park. Instantly feeling exposed I looked away and hoped that I didn't draw their attention. I had planned to hurl his teeth and snipped extremities over the cliff-edge, but this slightly altered as I didn't want to risk hanging about any longer, and the car occupants of the grey estate, getting a better look at me. It didn't really matter, as I would just have to get rid of them at a later date. For now, however, they were safely wrapped up in my handbag so there was no real urgency. I caught the train back home just as I had done before, making a slight detour to collect my car, which I had left parked close by. Handily for me, the train station was a relatively short distance away. I took the further precaution however of taking a cross-country route back to where I had left it. I really didn't need to be seen.

Once back at my car, I had such a strong temptation to check on the body and see how much was left. I wrestled with this in my mind, thinking that I should just leave it, you know…. Get going whilst the going was good... But then I gave in and wandered over to where I'd left him burning. To my absolute delight, there wasn't much to see, all that was left were his smouldering remnants. I covered them over with some mud and leaves from the forest floor and I felt such an overarching sense of achievement. I was good at this!

Superintendent Jo Gordon

I was so shocked when the call came through. The Boss, he had called me with an "opportunity" as he had put it. Of late, my area had been performing exceptionally well. I'd kept overtime down, crime down and detection rates up, and I really was seen as the blue-eyed girl. So much so, that due to a more "Collaborative Approach in UK Law Enforcement" (a far too much, an American concept for my liking), I had been selected to go on a secondment up North. He wanted me to go away for a couple of months, and for me, to showcase the 'forces', but he obviously meant MY best practice. I straight away thanked him for the opportunity but I couldn't go. Who would be in control whilst I was gone, and more importantly, who would look after my flock? I expressed my concerns, and his response was to put a fast tracker called Montgomery in. He would act up as my temporary replacement... "Have you heard of him?" He said.

Had I heard of him? Of course, I'd heard of him…. but only because he was shite! He'd run my tight little ship aground.

"Um …. Yes Sir. I have heard of him and I'm not entirely sure that he is exactly right for here."

"Well, it's a good job it's not your decision. You start Monday. I'll email you the details."

And with that, he was gone. I know it's rank and file, but bugger me! What? No discussion? No handover? And… Monty? …. Really? He's nice enough, but he and I are not even comparable! "Wet" is at best as how I would describe him. Sitting back in my chair, I know it's a done deal. There is nothing I can do about it, so I decide to take it for what it was; a massive compliment from the Boss. Who knows where this might lead...? Onwards and upwards as they say. I pop out to see Judy (my staff officer). She's nice enough, but she's another sap who's up the duff and now on restricted duties. Anyway, I tell her that I'll be away for a couple of months and that I'm going on a secondment. I then get off home, I've got a lot to do.

John

My focus has shifted of late. Yes, I know that I still need to work on her acquittal, but for now, getting Shelley back to being Shelley is my main goal. She has been transferred to a Prison Rehabilitation Unit, and for now they have no plans to move her back to HMP Lightbridge, so I'm happy with that. I have taken the girls in to see her a few times, and as strange as it sounds (considering how the prison visits affected them...) it's done them and of course her, the power of good.

The Unit is more akin to a care home than a prison facility. Most of the inmates are rather unwell. So, rest and recovery are what the Management focus upon. Shelley even has her own room with a view. Yes, the windows are barred, but it is much better than that segregation wing. I know they put her there for her own safety. Believing of course that her links to the police would have put her at risk. However, I think no matter what the other inmates might have done to her, all of that pales into insignificance, considering where we are now. The greatest risk ever posed to Shelley, was always going to be what she posed to herself. You only had to take a look at her ever-decreasing waistline and the self-harm marks on her arms, to know that her mental health was suffering. I had raised it, and I had thought that they were keeping her under close observation. Obviously not! I just wish I knew what the catalyst was. I know that there was an internal investigation into why that DS went to see her, and of course the referral to the IOPC, although neither has provided any clarity. I have tried my hardest to dig around, but most of my old contacts have been slow to come back to me. I can't blame them. We are all cut from the same cloth. None of us truly believe the convicted didn't do it. "There is no smoke without fire." I just wish they hadn't stepped back so far from me. One of them must know something. I bloody hate being a leper. I wish they'd realise that this was all down to bad luck, and none of it is catching!

Superintendent Jo Gordon

I am so bloody excited. This secondment feels like a holiday. I had my concerns to begin with, but since receiving my emailed instructions, I can totally see the benefits. The time away will do me some good and I've been given a massive opportunity. If all goes well, even after I retire, this one might serve me really well … "Guest Speaker" … Ooh… I like the sound of that!

I have been busy all weekend putting together a PowerPoint Presentation. I'm not sure if it's exactly what they want, but I have detailed my career path, as well as the strategies that I have implemented, and their subsequent results. It's important that they realise for this type of success, you have to have the right person at the top! ME!

I have also packed my case, (the biggest one in my luggage set). A girl has got to look her best you know! I intend to hit the town and take a few of them out. Really get to know them, if you know what I mean!

After heaving my supersized suitcase into the boot of my 19 plate Mercedes, I check my watch. I start the engine promptly, put it into gear, and with my foot on the gas, I roar up the road.   Shit! I really need to hurry up if I'm going to make my flight!

Josephine

I just couldn't believe it. They've what? I was listening to the radio and the news was on. The reporter stated that human remains had been discovered at a wooded area in Essex. The remains were apparently that of a local tradesman. Initially, I went cold, thinking that it was only a matter of time before I was arrested. When would there be a knock at the door? …. This train of thought however quickly evaporated, when the reporter went on to say that 'his wife was helping police with their enquiries.' We all know what they mean when they say… "Helping with enquiries."

They think she did it!

***

I couldn't work it out. How did they think she was involved? She had had nothing to do with it! Not that I cared. She hadn't supported her daughter, and in my mind, she was complicit in his crime anyway. Two for the price of one if she gets punished as well!

His discovery had made me question the effectiveness of my plan. What had I done wrong? Was it the plan or my execution of it…? How on earth was he identified? I had checked…. He was practically cinders.

I was on my way into work anyway, so I left a little earlier to see if there was anything else that I could find out. We had hard copies of all the daily newspapers, and surely there would be an article covering this. I needed to know more. I scanned every paper but there was nothing. The story must have broken after they had gone to print. I was most frustrated. I watched the news when I got in, but there was nothing. It was agonising. Did I dream it? I even asked Mum if she'd heard anything, but she didn't know what I was going on about. I remember she'd snapped at me. "Oh

Josephine, will you stop going on! Look I don't know anything about a body in the wood. Just eat your tea!"

It was a fretful wait, and for months there was nothing of note, other than that their enquiries were ongoing. Then bam! Reported in the Essex Local. In black and white, I read that the wife had been charged with his murder.

Josephine

For over a year I waited to find out what had happened. I didn't dare attend the court case for fear of being recognised. I had to be patient and make do with the tabloid snippets. The little bits of information as they reported the case. For motive, the Prosecutor pulled up the sexual-abuse case involving the deceased stepdaughter. They highlighted the unhappy marriage between the victim and the accused, and how he had manipulated her. He had forced her to support him, rather than her own flesh and blood. He controlled her through a fear of being left alone and destitute. They reported on how it was a premeditated act of revenge. How he'd been lured to his death in the woods. The Forensic Expert stated how the victim would have been approached from above, and he had surmised that he would have been bending down, and that how the stab wound, (although disguised by the fire) would have disabled the victim almost immediately.

The papers named her the "Black Widow". Her motive that they reported, was that she'd eliminated him to promote the survival of her offspring. They had detailed how she had disposed of his remains and almost made him unrecognisable, as there was nothing left, bar a serial numbered metal plate. This was unfortunately for her in his leg. It had been inserted there after an accident, back from when he was a teenager. The papers then went on to describe the fact that she'd driven his van to Beachy Head, left it there, and made it look like he'd committed suicide. They said that she had even reported him missing, so to make her crime all the more credible.

It would, (the reporter had said) have been the perfect crime, had she known about the metal plate, and if she'd not been spotted by a member of the public. Her slight frame and long blonde hair had been a key part of the witness identifying her, and placing her at the scene. I hadn't even considered it, but old Ferret Face's wife also looked childlike, and as fate would have it, she had a very close resemblance to me.

The final nail in her coffin was that she'd been to the petrol station in the days preceding the murder. The attendant remembered her filling up a jerrycan. The 'SORRY' suicide note was actually in her handwriting, AND she had no alibi. That's the problem with being married to a controlling male. You don't work, you don't have any friends, and therefore no one to vouch for the fact, that you were actually at home, and ironing his smalls on a Thursday afternoon in the late spring. And not committing his brutal murder!

The jury convicted her and she was sentenced to a minimum of 30 years. Did I feel remorse? Was I sorry that someone else took the blame? Not in the slightest. She was every bit as complicit in his crimes, and by not standing up for her daughter, she had got everything that she deserved.

John

It was a great visit today; she's looking more like my Shelley. Her eyes are less bloodshot and she seems much happier in herself. I know she doesn't remember anything of the "incident", and so we obviously don't know why she did it, and so far, unfortunately, even with some therapy, she hasn't been able to recall a thing.

I have seen the photos and the Prison Officer's Body-Worn Camera Footage, and I know that she must have made that decision in a moment of utter madness. She never wanted to die. At first, I found it hard to watch. From looking at the photographs as to where she'd been initially discovered, I surmised that she had wrapped a sheet around the top bunk of the bed, popped the noose around her neck, and slipped off the bottom bunk.

On the body-worn camera footage, you can hear the excitement and fear in the young officer's voice. He was just doing his checks and on looking through the wicket into Shelley's cell, he screams for help. Him and another officer rush in. The footage is muffled and jolty but you can make out that they are cutting her down. The younger officer does the cutting and gets her free. His voice is heightened as he says "Shit! That's the first time I've done that!". This is then followed up by clearly an older officer who says back to him... "Well, it won't be your last, Son!"

She's got froth at her mouth and I can make out reddening or scratches around her neck. She had clearly changed her mind, causing these as she must have been thrashing about as she tried desperately to cling on to life. The images are blurry, but the audio is clear. The older officer, he struggles to get her jaw unclamped to administer the CPR. He is frantic, and after what seems like forever, the paramedics turn up and they take over.

I've not shown the footage to Shelley as I think it will be too distressing for her. It's strange as throughout my career I've been to numerous suicide calls. I've cut them down; I've done the CPR, and I have witnessed the lover's pacts. You know, the ones where you discover their liquidised remains, only after the neighbour reportedly has a fly infestation, and no amount of air freshener can mask the pungent smell in their communal hallway. I have comforted the bankrupt trader's wife, after he has jumped from their penthouse apartment. His life leaving no more than a stain on the pavement below, for an unlucky council-worker to then scrub clean.

It's work, you process it. You fill in a form, make the right calls, and attend the Coroners Court. Once the day is over, you forget all about it, and you go home to your family. But what do you do when it is your family? How do you go on to process that? I know we were lucky. She survived. I know she's in the best place right now, and under the care of the Psychiatric Team, but it's all so tough.

I'm still trying to mount an appeal. I still want to ask her about the note. Was it the 'Enclosed' contents that sent her over the edge? I have so many questions but I'm not sure she's strong enough to answer. I also know for sure, that I recognise that bloody handwriting. I have been wracking my mind for over a week now but still, I cannot place it.

Josephine

After Ferret Face, my court trips became rather fruitless. Don't get me wrong, I'm not complaining. I'm glad the British Judiciary is functioning as it should. Their victims are finally getting the justice that they deserve.

John

I contacted Jackie at the Prison to ask her if she knew anything of the provenance of the letter, and the missing enclosed part. She said she would look into it, but I'm not holding out too much hope. I have also had my ear to the ground at work, and apparently, the DS who visited Shelley has concerns over the safety of her conviction. I know that it's only the rumour mill for now, but I'll take any help I can get. I have my fingers crossed, and I hope that she is committed to finding out the truth.

Josephine

For three weeks, I followed the trial. I had annual leave that needed using up, so I took a punt and ended up in Exeter. I'd told Mum that I was on a course, and it wasn't too much of a stretch (for her to believe me), as I'd recently started an educational programme at the library. It was my boss's idea. She had a plan that I should get a degree in Library Science. I liked her faith and optimism in me. It was so nice to have someone in my corner.

John

We have finally had a breakthrough. I walked in today and Shelley was up (sat in a chair), dressed, and seemed much more like herself. She had had a good session with the counsellor, and it really showed. It's a double-edged sword this place. I want her to get better, but if she does, and is deemed fit, she'll be transferred back to the prison. I really can't let that happen, so I decide that today is the day that I show her the letter.

"Baby, take a look, do you remember this?"
She turns the letter in her hands, and having read it, she asks.
"Where's the rest of it? It says Enc."
"I don't know. But do you remember it?"
"No, I've never seen it before... Who is M?"
"I was kinda hoping that you knew. Look at the handwriting. I'm sure I recognise it."
After pondering it only a slight moment she replies...

"Actually, now you say that, so do I. Oh my god, John, it's my mum's!"

"What? Is it? Are you sure? Your mum's is more fluid and curlier…"

"No, not Mum Mum. I mean my real mum. Go home and look at the diary. I'm sure of it."

"Oh my god Shel, I think you're right... I see it now..."
I can feel a tingling come all over me…. I need to get home. I need to confirm if the writing is the same.
"Baby, this might be the break we need. I've got to go...."

And with that, I kiss her gently and I rush out of the door… For the first time in a long while, I feel like I'm getting somewhere, and I finally have real hope.

Shelley

I'm tired, and I've not slept a wink all night. The words from the note, that John had shown me, have been going around and around in my head. Was it my mum? My biological mother, I mean. Was the dead man my rapist father? I wished that John would just call me, and let me know. Did the writing match up? My thoughts are only broken by one of the staff members coming in to check on me.

"Are you getting up for breakfast? Your session is in an hour."

I nod my head. God, I long for the day when I'm in control of my own schedule. I miss long baths, runs in the open-air, and even the pain of a spinning class. I just want to tuck my girls into bed, read them their bedtime stories. Make gingerbread, daisy chains, wipe the tears from their cheeks, and bandage their bloody knees.

I want so much to be free from this place!

Josephine

So, the case in Exeter, was the prosecution of a paedophile ring that had preyed on young boys. Five of them in total, and all of them old enough to have been their victim's grandfathers. The ringleader owned a toy shop in the town, and it was the perfect front, to a very sordid backroom.

Geraint Pike was his name. He was a skinny little man and he had looked so frail, stood there in the dock. He had worked hard to portray this façade of being too weak to have committed, or even instigated any sort of crime. Especially the type of crime as heinous as this.

His MO was enticement, and it was the oldest trick in the book. Although, rather than using the traditional promise of seeing a puppy, or the receiving of sweets; he had actually lured his victims (all young boys), by giving them the latest and most desirable of toys and games. Bigtrack, Nintendo Gameboys, Sonic Mountain Quest... All of the latest gadgets and he had them all. He had them set up in his backroom. He also provided spiked refreshments too. He would let the boys play with whatever their hearts desired, and all the while the drugs would be taking effect. Then when they were incapacitated, he and his sick friends, they would rape and sexually assault them.

It was wicked. The boys, all from poor and disadvantaged backgrounds, either didn't tell, weren't believed, or weren't sure what had actually happened. Either way, all of this vileness went on for years. It was only after one brave lad spoke out, that they were stopped. He was not only believed, but when he had been examined, these men's perversions had become instantly apparent. It was sickening to discover the extent of his internal injuries; all inflicted upon him by these depraved monsters.

As I sat in the gallery, all I wanted to do was weep, as I heard all of the medical evidence that was put forward. The Expert Witness, he not only covered the physical injuries, but also the psychological damage that they had inflicted too.

His co-defendants, (the other four monsters) all pleaded guilty to their involvement, but this creature, he decided to put his victims through a harrowing court case, and by some cruel twist of fate, he was acquitted.

I had my next target. Those boys deserved justice.

John

I had to go up into the loft to find the diary. After we had pulled out of the house sale, anything from Shelley's past was boxed up, and put up and out of the way. So, having made my way through the dusty cobwebs, I found the old Volvic box, and nestled within it was her mother's diary. Opening up the first page and even in the dull light, that the single lightbulb hanging above provided, I knew that I had something, the handwriting although clearly more juvenile, was definitely a match!

Josephine

Fortunately for me, the townsfolk of Exeter were none too keen on the local toy shop owner's antics. And acquitted or not, his premises had been vandalised. Without a safe home nor work premises, he had no reason to stay. He certainly wouldn't be picking up from where he left off, his days of living in Exeter were well and truly over.

I knew he had moved, but I needed to find out where he had actually relocated to. It took me a fair few months, but I finally uncovered it. I really should have been a detective; my skills were wasted at the Library! I'd got chatting to the local postman, and he had rather helpfully given me the postal redirection address. I had asked him for it on the pretence that Pike was my uncle, and my father (his brother), was gravely ill in hospital. I went all sob story... "and his dying wish is to see his brother...." I had looked innocent enough, and I wasn't sure if the postie had believed me, or he was just sloppy about giving away people's personal information. It wouldn't happen in today's data protection mad society, but that was the '90's for you… Or maybe, he had seen the press coverage of the case, and he knew exactly who Pike was, and he was hoping, that I did indeed have darker intentions. Either way, I got what I wanted - a location, so all I needed now was a plan.

Josephine

Having looked up the address that I was given, I discovered that to my absolute delight, that Pike had moved literally around the corner from my own home. It was a part of the town that I wasn't overly familiar with, but it didn't matter, as there were to be no more six-hour drives, that I would have to contend with. This was fate giving me a helping hand, once again. I was destined to deal with this one, and as I knew I'd not be able to appeal to him sexually; this time I really had to get creative, and think outside of the box.

John

Jackie called me from the Prison, but unfortunately, she hadn't been able to locate a thing. My hopes were a little dashed but I still felt optimistic. DS Cooper was still an untapped source. If Shelley's biological mother was the author, there was no reason that she would not have sent a duplicate copy to the police, as she had said. I needed to know what to do, and whether I should also disclose the diary. I rang Larry and left a message for him to call.

Josephine

I left it a while as I didn't want to spook Pike, and I also had a lot of studying to do. To satisfy my boss at the Library, I had started a NVQ and to my surprise, I was actually quite enjoying it. My mind was temporarily occupied elsewhere, so I was a little shocked when he wandered by chance into the library, to take shelter on a rainy afternoon. I was busy dealing with a reservation, and I was desperately trying to sort out the paperwork, as it needed to be transferred from our Central Library. As soon as I'd completed my task, I turned to look for him, but to my disappointment, I watched as he boarded a bus just outside. Inwardly I was scolding the old dear who'd had me sort out her query. He was there, I had him. It would have been the perfect of chance meetings.

Josephine

So, there I was, in full flow of my rather funny puppet version of Old Macdonald's Farm. I had begun to include this in the Library's Toddler Rhyme Time Sessions. This type of foolery was completely out of my comfort zone, as were the conversations that I had to have with the parents afterwards. However, it was a new initiative by Imogen, (my boss) to get the younger readers in, and to create a sense of community amongst their mothers. It was at this session, that I had spotted him. He was sat at the very edge of the circle, looking very much like a kind old man. A little later on I had watched him cooing over one of the youngsters, and striking up a conversation with their mother. Instantly I wanted to run over, and to warn her about him, but I couldn't. I had to watch and wait, knowing that his and my time was yet to come.

John

Larry called me back, and we discussed what I'd got, and in his opinion, unfortunately, he thought I had nothing. It was a blow, but I understood what he meant. I had been so caught up with it, and the prospect of it, giving us the means to launch an appeal, I hadn't really looked at its content. There was nothing in that letter, that said Shelley was innocent. All he suggested, was that I make contact with the DS who had visited Shelley, to see if she knew anything of the duplicate copy. I had mentioned that I'd already tried Jo, and he had laughed at me…. "…and you're expecting her to help? How? She's all about getting a result that one. I'm not even sure if she really cares much for the actual truth!"

After hanging up, I thought about what he'd said, and so I put a call into DS Cooper.

Josephine

Pike had become quite a regular at the Library. He was like clockwork. He was always, and without fail present for Rhyme Time, the Summer Readathon, etc, etc. Anytime really, when children were the library's target audience, there he would be. He'd help their mothers on, or off the bus, and often provide a Kleenex, just at the right moment. He was clearly very skilled at his craft. I would give him that. To them, he was simply a kind old man, and not in the least bit predatory. He took his time, earning their trust, as sooner or later, he knew that he would be rewarded with their most prized possessions. He really was a sick and perverse old man.

John

I was surprised at just how receptive DS Cooper was. She had been really interested in the note. I had decided not to mention anything of the diary, or of my suspicions that the note's author was Shelley's biological mother. I knew myself, that police officers are fundamentally lazy, and if she had read the diary, and interpreted the rape as motive for the murder, she may have looked no further. No, it was better that I disclosed the minimal of details, and then she would remain focused in her efforts of finding the duplicate copy of the missing "Enclosed", and uncovering the truth.

Josephine

I was very fortunate. Having sat through the court case, I knew exactly the type of victim that Pike was attracted to. His preference was for eight-year-old boys. All of his previous victims, had been white with dark hair, so I needed to get the bait just right. I had got a picture of a very fresh-faced boy from a clothing catalogue, and I framed it. I popped the framed picture onto the reservations desk, and I made sure that it was visible to all who left the library. It was as simple as that... And Pike noticed him straight away. Remarking... "Oh he's a very handsome lad. He reminds me of my grandson." I carried on with my task of stamping his books, and I pretended not to hear him.

"Sorry, did you say something?"

"Yes, the young lad. Is he yours?"

"Not mine as such, he's my godson. Yes, he's lovely."

"Does he come here to see you then?"

"The Library? No... Books are not really his thing. Climbing trees and football are more his passion, and those new handheld gaming things!"

"A true boy then..."

I could practically see him salivating. Disgusting old pervert!

"Yes, you could say that. I feel for him really, surrounded by women. His father died last year, and it's been really hard for his mother without a male role model in his life."

"Oh really, that's awful. Well, I love a game of football. I'm not so agile as to climb trees, and I think you mean a Gameboy. The handheld gaming thing.... so, if you ever need a hand...."

"Ah, that's really kind of you. I've got him next weekend actually, so I might just take you up on that." I say this whilst smiling at him...

"Really? Well, I'm quite a regular here now, and you've got my details on my library record. I'd absolutely love to be of assistance, if you need any help."

The smile shone across his face, and I could see the delight in his eyes. He really thought that he was on his way to securing his next victim. My approach had been a stroke of genius, and he had fallen for it hook, line and sinker.

Josephine

I knew it was a long-shot, and I had just one chance at this, so I had to get it right. My plan was to lure Pike to a wooded area on the outskirts of the town. (Yes, I know, another wooded area. But if it ain't broke, don't fix it!) I would set up a picnic blanket, snacks, and a football on a grassy area nearby, and then I would get Pike to venture into the woods, to go and find "Sammy," who would be conveniently climbing the trees. Careful planning was to be the key, so I needed all of my provisions there in advance. I also needed to be sure that the woods were remote enough, to execute my plan without being disturbed.

DS Rachel Cooper

It was such a shock when John called me. I thought I was seen as the enemy. Firstly, I'm the one that secured the evidence against his wife, and then after my visit to the prison, she tries to take her own life. I still can't work out what the catalyst was for that. I have debriefed that day and our conversation, over and over in my head. I know I annoyed her asking about the case, but when I left her, she seemed angry. She had fight. She was certainly not in my opinion, the least bit suicidal.

Josephine

I wake up on the woodland floor. It was dark and I felt wet. I try to right myself, but as I go to move, I can feel a searing pain on my left side. My face is also stinging. I'm not sure if it's mud, congealed blood, or both, as there is an overpowering smell of iron in the air. That metallic scent, it took me back to the butcher's shop that I used to go to with Mum, to buy my dad's favourite black pudding. It had the exact same smell, minus the hint of wood shavings, and it briefly catapulted me back to a much happier, and simpler life. How I wished Dad were still alive.

I attempt to move again, but I really hurt, and I wonder if I have done something serious. I try to work out what has happened, and then I remember. Shit! I was dealing with Pike. I make an effort to recall the events of the day, and I try to understand, as to why it is that I have found myself on the floor. I begin to panic. Actually, where is Pike? I feel about at ground level, as it's too dark for me to see properly, and then I feel something. It's a leg, definitely a leg. Still in pain I try to move away, trying hard to remove myself from any potential danger, and then I find it. My handbag. Most of the contents are missing, but fishing around, I find the lighter that I had placed in it earlier in the day. With my hand shaking, it takes three attempts to get it to spark, but then finally I can see. Sprawled out to my left, is the motionless body of Pike. I don't know how, but I had done it again, he was definitely dead. My only problem, well, not the only problem... I still had a body to dispose of... but the most pressing of all problems, was that it was well past ten o'clock at night, and my mum would be worried. I knew that I really had no time to deal with him, or any of the mess. I also felt and looked like, I had done ten rounds with Mike Tyson. My mum would have plenty of questions for me when I got home, and I knew, that I had to have the answers.

DS Rachel Cooper

On the quiet, I have started to ask around about any potential "new evidence." I had already looked on the system, but there was nothing noted. I looked at both the paper and electronic case files, but nothing had been recorded on the MG6 series. I hadn't really expected there to be, as from what I could tell, this new evidence was supposedly received post-conviction. I even asked the guys at the property store, to see if they had had any new evidence recently booked in. They too came up empty-handed.

I started to think that there was nothing to find, when a male officer, pops his head in and around my office door.
"Sarge, you got a minute?"
"It's Rachel, we don't bother with all that in CID... What can I do for you?" I say this with a friendly tone and with a big smile across my face. It's rare to have a

visitor to the Cold Cases Department... It's like we are just as forgotten about, as the unsolved crimes that we investigate!

"Come in, come in..."

"Well, it's probably nothing, but one of the station officers were saying that you were asking about any new evidence, that had come in for that Body in the Wood job. The one that the forensic bird got done for."

"Ok yes, go on."

"Well, something did come in. I was night duty and covering the desk and this woman, she comes in with a carrier bag full of stuff, and she tells me to give it to the Gaffer."

"What carrier bag? What was in it? What did you do with it?" I start to fire questions at him in my excitement over what he's just told me.

"Well, I gave it to her. Ma'am Gordon... She was well interested. I don't know what was in there, but she told me to arrest her..."

"Really? ... Well, Ok, so did you? What happened?"

I'm finding the difficulty in getting information out of this lad, bloody frustrating.

"No 'cos, Ma'am rushes past me and I do follow, but by the time we get down again, she's gone. Ma'am even puts it out on the radio, but she's already vanished."

"And when was this?"

"I dunno, but I can work it out. I just need to look at my old pocketbook."

"Ok and did you get a look in the bag?"

"To be honest no, but Ma'am was definitely interested in it."

"Ok thanks, thanks for letting me know. Sorry I didn't catch your name."

"It's Josh, Sarge. (*DS Cooper smiles again at his formality.*) Sorry Rachel, Josh Martin." *He colours up, embarrassed.*

"Ok, Josh Martin, thanks for that. When you have a moment, please can you give me the date of when all of this happened?"

"Yes, no problem Sarge... anything else?"

"No that's great, and Josh... It's Rachel."

"Erm yes sorry, ok then I'll email you then."

"Perfect."

Josh closes the door behind him, and I begin to feel the excitement bubbling from deep within me... I think to myself... I finally have a lead!!

Josephine

I make it home. It is too late for me to do anything now, and anyway I know that I'm definitely not strong enough. By the faint light of the lighter, I had nipped back to my car and collected a torch. This at least allowed me to see what devastation awaited me. It also enabled me to tidy away the picnic things that were still scattered on the grass. I still wasn't sure exactly what had happened, but I knew we had been in the wooded area. I had been directing him towards "Sammy" and then he turned, and he asked me was I sure that he'd not wandered off? I remembered part of the conversation.

"Are you sure you should have let him go this far alone? Not everyone is as they seem, you know... In this day and age, you've got to take more care...." He's busy trying to educate me, as he is wandering further into the woods. It was like he was preaching at me.

Questioning my ability to look out for a child. A child that didn't even exist! Well, his "concern for Sammy", it was like him lighting a touchpaper...

"Like you, you mean?"

He turned, clearly shocked by my response.

"What do you mean by that?"

"You know very well; I've seen you at the Library. I've seen you cooing at the kids, getting your "in" with their mothers... I know you; I know your type. I know what you did."

Then it dawns on him. There was no "Sammy." The fear in his eyes began glistening like beacons against the darkness of the wood.

"Look, I don't know who you are, or what you think you know, but I didn't do it. I was acquitted. I've come here to start over. Get a new life. I'm innocent!"

"Innocent! I've seen you. You only get the bus so that you get to talk to them on their way home. Little gifts here, little gifts there. You are a predator. I've seen it. I've watched you. Gerri, that young mum. How long did it take you to realise that she is single, and has boys aged seven and two? She told me; you turned up on her doorstep with a football, and a brand-new bloody Gameboy!"

He doesn't say a word, he tries to push past me but he's too late. I've already got my hand on the knife, and I stab him. I remember the blood, and it splattering me in the face but then it goes blank, and I have no further memory. The only explanation that I have, is that he must have fallen on me, or assaulted me which resulted in my blacking out. Either way, my mission was accomplished. He was dead.

DS Rachel Cooper

I must have refreshed my emails at least 100 times that morning. After Josh's revelation, I was keen to look into whatever this was. Ma'am was still away on her secondment, jolly or whatever it was, so I didn't want to bother her, and I'm not really sure how helpful she'd be anyway. She truly believed that there was no link to the other cases. She had got her conviction, so in her mind, that was the end of it. It didn't sit right with me, however. Something was amiss.

Anyway, eventually at 14:10 hours, in came his email. If only I had checked his roster, I could have saved myself all that clicking... and got some actual work done. He wasn't due back in until the late turn, which was a two o'clock start, so he'd obviously emailed as soon as he was back in. Anyway, 21st March was the date that I needed to focus on. I was all fired up. At last, I had a starting point!

Josephine

Mum was on at me as soon as I had got through the front door. I had tried to use some water and a tissue to clean myself up, but it hadn't achieved much.
"Mary, Mother of God! What on earth has happened to you? Josephine, is that blood?" I try to shy away from her...
"Yes, Mum! No... nothing really, I'm fine!"
"Well, you don't look fine... What has happened? Someone attack you? You had an accident? What? Tell me!"
I had concocted a story on the way home whilst driving back. I needed it to sound convincing so I had practiced it out loud...
"I'm not sure really, I was late leaving the library. I had wanted to get a few bits finished off, and once I was done, I had decided to take a shortcut through the park, and back to the car... I think I was jumped from behind.

I don't really remember. I just woke up on the floor and now, here I am."

"Well, did they rob you? Did they .... you know?"

"RAPE ME, MUM?!" The words erupt out of my mouth angrily, and without me even realising. I had previously told her that I had been raped but she didn't listen then, so why on earth was it her concern now?

"No! They haven't raped me." I say this sarcastically.

"Oh, that's good then." She looks genuinely relieved. Although, I don't think it is because of her overarching concern for me. It was probably her worrying about the shame of another pregnancy, that she would then feel compelled to hide.

"Right then, well, I'll get you a nice sweet tea and you can clean yourself up. Do you want me to call the police?"

"Police!! Um ... NO MUM!!" I practically scream this at her.

"What? Oh no! You've got to report it. Look at the state of you. Cuts and bruises, and you are practically soaked in blood. Do you want me to check you over?" Mum's Irish accent is so strong. It always is when she is panicking... I'm not wanting to get into an argument, or have her realise that most of the blood was his. So, I appease her by saying that I would call into the Police Station in the morning. This obviously... also gave me the perfect excuse to go out early and to sort everything out. All I needed right now was a hot bath and a good night's sleep. I hoped it would be enough to heal me ahead of all the work, that I needed to get done tomorrow. God, how I ached!

Josephine

I was absolutely exhausted. Not just physically, but mentally too. Had this been my near-miss? I wasn't the type of person to be reckless. I knew this had to be my last one. I wasn't a psychopath; I wasn't driven by some perverse reason to kill. No, I was just trying to make the world a better place. I wanted their victims to finally be able to sleep peacefully again at night.

The next morning, I looked in the bathroom mirror. I had a black eye, and grazes on my forehead. I was shocked at just how much my head had actually bled, when really the severity of my injuries had been no more than a paper cut. I had intended to cover it over with concealer, so that my day ahead wasn't thwarted by a do-gooder, wanting to know if I were alright. However, I heard Mum shuffling about in the next room. She was clearly awake, and she would want to know why I'd covered it up, if I were going to the Police

Station to report it. Instead, I shoved the limited makeup that I owned into my bag, and decided I'd make myself up after I had left the house.

I came down to the kitchen. It was still early, so the sun was just getting established for the day. Mum was in her dressing gown and was busy fussing, stood over by the kettle and the toaster.
"I heard you, so I thought I best get up. Do you want breakfast before you go?" I made no sound, I just looked at her. I was still trying to summon up the stamina that I knew I needed, just to get through the day. My side was still really hurting and my muscles felt stiff.
"I think you should, who knows how long it will take you…. Oh, and I was going to wash this…" She says this shoving my dress back at me. She had put it in a carrier bag. "But then I thought better of it. They can do amazing things these days. I read it in my 'Woman's

Realm'... There's all sorts of evidence.... fibres, um... other stuff... I can't remember now..."

"Oh, right? Ok, Mum, thank you." I never realised that my mum was so on the ball. Unwittingly however, she'd helpfully reminded me to get rid of that dress.

I sat at the table, and she presented me with a mug of tea and some white buttered toast. I had got up feeling nauseous but actually, I think I needed it to settle my stomach.

"So what time are you going? Do you want me to come?"
"Um... no Mum, I'll be fine... Probably in a bit. I want to get it over and done with. You know, whilst it's all still fresh in my head."
"I still think you would be better going via A&E, just to get checked out properly."
"No honestly, Mum. It's just a little bruising. I must have fallen funny that's all."

"Well, if you're sure. I can't make you. You are just like your father. He had your stubborn streak."

"It's not stubborn, Mum! I just don't want to waste their time. I'm fine..."

I finish my last mouthful of toast and I swig it down with the tea.

"Right then, let's get this over with."

By 6:45 am, I have left the house, and I'm back in my car and on route back to the Woods.

Shelley

John brought the girls in with him today, and it was just wonderful. They had their colouring books, and I was helping Heidi with the colouring in of a rainbow unicorn, that was to be her latest masterpiece. It's funny, although the girls have aged, I still see them as my babies. I find it amazing that Maggie can now read. It still seems like it was only last week that I was taking her to the local playgroup. God, I would do anything to get back all that lost time.

John and I had spoken in code for some of the visit. We were not wanting the girls to hear, but it seems that he has passed the note to that DS Rachel. I'm not sure what it will achieve, but I suppose if they did get given a copy, and it is at the Station; she is probably the best placed to find it. When she came to the Prison, I got the impression that she wanted to revisit the case. Although, not that I remember much of our conversation, and I still don't know why I did what I did. It really must have been a split-second decision. I have so much to live for, and in a moment of absolute madness, I nearly chucked that all away. God! What if I had succeeded? My poor babies... Shame flushes over me, as I think of the further horrors that I nearly inflicted upon them. Not only the girls, but on John, and Mum and Dad too. I have been discussing this recently with my support worker. She has been trying to stop me from blaming myself, but who else is there to blame? Anyway, John didn't elaborate, but he said he'd let me know if there were any developments as soon as he knew.

Josephine

I make it back to the woodland, where I had awoken not 8 hours since. It was quiet, eerie; and I felt uneasy like it was the scene from a horror film. I kept looking over my shoulder. I was sure that I was being watched. His van was still parked up along the road. My goodness, how he must have looked forward to yesterday. He really thought it was his lucky day. The dirty old bastard.

I didn't waste any time; I already had the tools of my trade readily packed and accessible in the boot of my car. I walked over, and into the shaded area where I'd left him. He was still there posed exactly the way he must have fallen. I still can't recall exactly how it happened, but the knife, it must have nicked something vital, and he must have bled-out pretty quickly. Maybe instinctively he had fought in the short moments before his death? That's the only explanation that I have for him having knocked me out. Either that, or he fell on me and I hit my head? I was so glad that I had awoken when I did. There would have been no way that I could have explained an even later home time to Mum. Assault story or not.

I was well versed in my technique as I performed the necessary extractions. I also dug a shallow sort of grave, and I rolled him onto the tarpaulin. As always, I then doused him (and this time my dress) with the petrol and set them both alight. The way the flames instantly took hold was so satisfying, and it didn't take long for his corpse to be burning brightly. I still haven't fathomed why in the three cremations that I have done to date; that no one has called the fire brigade. Was I just lucky, or did no one care anymore? I know I'd picked my spots for being remote, but you'd always pass some faraway dwelling on route, you know tucked out of the way. Maybe that's it. The type of person who moves to a remote location, does it to keep to themselves. They don't want to be part of society, and that includes not calling up the emergency services, because someone has lit an inferno in their local woods. Either way, I don't really care about their reasons. Their reluctance to be public-spirited has so far worked out in my favour.

I had done a last cursory look about the woodland floor to make sure that I had not missed anything, just before I headed off, and it was a very good job that I did. I had nearly left behind the treasured picture that I had of my dad. I always carried it in my bag. I had done so since he had left me. It was both a reminder of him and it also made me feel safe. It was old and dog-eared, and at a quick glance, its colouring resembled a rotting leaf. It must have fallen out last night. Anyway, I picked it up with a sigh, and then I made my way over to Pike's van.

It was the first time that I had been in his van, and it smelled old and musty, just like him. On climbing in I immediately noticed something in the passenger footwell. Something wrapped in a football print paper.

I leaned down and picked it up. It was a box. I read the card.

To Sammie, I hope you enjoy this.
Love Uncle Geraint xx.

Ripping open the brightly coloured paper, I knew exactly what it was, and I was right. A brand-new Gameboy. My god, he really hadn't learned his lesson. Just as well that I got to him when I did.

I put the key in the ignition and I'm immediately off. I travel down the motorway to dump his van, and to stage this one last suicide. It's my third and final time. I have decided that last night's very near-miss, was a clear signal. I had to find another way.

Josephine

During the journey, my mind had been occupied. So, without even realising it, I had arrived at the all too familiar South Downs. The motorway had been a blur, I had navigated solely on autopilot. I drove into the car park, and I hoped that it would be quiet today and that I wouldn't be spotted. I could ill afford another member of the public, coming forward with a description of a petite female, and being at the same location. This time I knew there was no one else who was obvious, nor deserving to take the fall. Fate would never be kind enough a second time around, or third in this case. There were no other vehicles present, apart from an old Mini Cooper, which was parked up in the corner. I checked and couldn't see any occupants, so I quickly exited the van, ensuring I left it unlocked, with Pike's wallet left in the glove box. After a few days of being parked up there, I was sure that it would pique somebody's interest. No note this time, as I thought I would leave it up to the local bobbies to put the pieces of the puzzle together.

It was a lovely day at the coast. There was a light breeze, so I decided to take a slow amble from the top of the cliff, and down and into the town. I did this not only so that I could appreciate my surroundings; the long grass, and the yellow and purple flowers dotted about, but also because I hurt. My body was still in agony from whatever had happened to me last night.

Rather than head straight to the train station, as I had done on all the previous occasions, I decided to head to the beach. I needed to re-centre myself. I think I was still in shock, and as I walked down towards the pier, I was comforted by memories of me holding my dad's hand. I smiled thinking about how we'd eaten a 'Mr Whippy' ice-cream on the last occasion that we had visited there together. Sadly, that was a long, long time ago now.

I walked across the shingle and I sat to the edge of the beach, propping myself up by the sea defences. I then watched the tide come in. I let my thoughts also come and go, mimicking the sea's froth over the pebbles. This had to be my last one.

Shelley

As peculiar as it sounds, I felt free at the unit. I knew that the windows were still barred, as their shadows acted as a constant reminder, casting themselves on the floor. This however didn't seem to matter to me, as I no longer felt that my mind was as imprisoned as it once was.

I would go for my daily sessions and just talk and talk. I had had therapy before, but nothing like this. Maybe I had had a greater form of mental illness, than I'd ever previously appreciated. The realisation back when I was a teen, and what I had learnt about my start in life, I knew that it had left me with scars, but I never realised just how deep the cuts actually were. I had also recently been given the OK, to start limited exercise. The damage that I had caused physically to myself had been great. I had actually managed to break my neck. Luckily for me, however, the vertebrae had fused, and I was finally healed. I had to be careful, but at least I was up and about properly, rather than just being dressed and sat in the chair. It felt amazing. I was desperate to get back to being me, but at the back of my mind, I knew that if I improved too much, or too soon, I'd be back at HMP Lightbridge, and the harsh reality of this, was the bitterest of all the pills, that I now had to take.

Josephine

I had eventually made it back home. It was past my usual 7 pm home time, and I had been out of the house for well over 12 hours. The makeup that I'd used to conceal my black-eye, and the cuts to my face had long since worn off. My war-wounds were clearly visible for all to see. My key had turned in the front door lock, and Mum was there, stood in the hallway as soon as I came in. She had her usual uniform on of a floral pinny, and the house smelt of baking. It's what she always did if she were upset, or concerned about something.

"Oh Josephine, you've been out all day. I've been so worried. What did the police say? Did you do a statement? Have you been to the hospital? Are they going to catch him?" Her Irish accent accentuated the words, as she fired questions at me, as if she were a machine gun.
"Mum, calm down, I'm fine. Look it's all sorted."

"What? So, have they got him? Oh Josephine, look what he did to your face!"

"Look, Mum... Please... it's all sorted, nothing to worry about."

"What's all sorted? Did they get him?"

I could sense the annoyance in her voice, but I couldn't tell her anymore. One important thing that I had learnt whilst growing up, is that the less you say, the less likely it is, that you will be found out as a liar...

"I don't know Mum. We'll just leave it for now, anyway what's for tea? I'm starving."

Mum sensing that she was getting nowhere, and as her default setting was more of a practical one, she switched straight over to her 'everyday functional mode'.

"Ah yes, it's in the oven. Your favourite, Toad-in-the-Hole."

"Thanks, Mum, let me just clean myself up and get changed and I'll be in for it."

And that was that, Mum never said another word about the assault. Well, not to me anyway.

John

I saw her name flash up on the phone's display, so I picked it up straight away, although I was still very hesitant. Was she really someone I could trust? Or was she just another one of Jo's puppets and Jo, although conveniently hidden, was she still pulling the strings?

"Hello"
"Um… Hi John, it's Rachel Cooper. Have you got a minute?"
"Yes. Hi Rachel…" Obviously, I knew it was her….
"What can I do for you?"
"Look, I'm still looking into the letter, and what if anything has been received… I did come across something a little strange… and thought you might be able to shed some light?"
"Ok, go on" …. My stomach is churning. What has she found?

"Well, there is the letter that you brought to me, and there is a photo that we found at your house... It was in evidence, the one which showed the deceased... and...well... It appears to me, that it has very similar writing on. What was the origin of that photo? I've looked on file, but the prepared statement doesn't really give me much to go on, and in interview, any questions put to your wife, she no commented...."

"Ah ok, well, to be honest, I'm not entirely sure, but the photo I believe was left with my wife when she was abandoned. You know she's a foundling, right?"

"Um, was she? I'm not sure I did! So, the M, could be what? Her mother?"

"Could be, I suppose. Look, can we meet?"

"Yes, sure, but I'm tucked up on another job at the mo. I just had five minutes, so I wanted to touch base. Look, I'll call you next week to arrange."

And with that, she has ended the call. This left me a little uneasy. That was very much of a Jo thing to do. Call up, get what she wants, and then go. I much prefer a face-to-face conversation. It's so much easier to judge a person, when you can actually observe their body language. Should I have gone to her? I just didn't know, but as Larry said, I had nothing. I've just got to trust her, and leave it to her to do the digging. It's not like I have an all-areas access pass these days. I am briefly saddened, as I think about what I have lost career-wise, but then that's nothing compared to my personal life, and that is what I wanted back more than anything. Anyway, the job's fucked, so it could do one for all I cared about it these days.

DS Rachel Cooper

The 21st March had been a bit of a dead-end. I had gone down all of the usual routes of CCTV and witnesses. Josh had told me that an unknown female had definitely attended that day, and that she had given something over for Ma'am Gordon. He had described her reaction as initially panicked, but as he hadn't bothered to look at what he was handing over to her, it didn't really assist me. What type of a Copper doesn't have a quick peek at what they have been given? He's certainly not one that I'll be petitioning to join me in CID! You need to be a bit bloody inquisitive!

The CCTV at the Front Office had over-written, as had the camera outside, so I really had no idea who our mystery caller was, nor what her little gift-bag had contained. Maybe I would have to bite the bullet and call Ma'am, but I am fully aware that I am still not back in her good books, and officially I have been told to leave this one alone. I needed another angle…. I think hard and I realise that Montgomery is still caretaking at the moment, and he's using Ma'am's office. As he's only 'Acting Superintendent', I wonder if he's cleared it out? I walk up the steps to the landing where the Senior Management Team reside, and to my absolute joy, I see Judy sat outside the Office. She is heavily pregnant and performing the role of Staff Officer. Judy was in my intake; we had joined together. How did I miss that she was so close to the Boss?

"Hey Hun, how are you? I didn't know you were expecting?"
"Yeah, not long to go now. Wasn't planned but… you know."

I don't really know. I have never had any real want for children, so planned or not, I would never be expecting. It really is the quickest way to ruin your career in my opinion… And I really did join this job to make a difference. I don't share this with Judy however. I just smile at her and nod…

"Hun, is he in?"

"Montgomery? No, he's out for a meeting with the Bigwigs. Do you need to see him?"

"Actually no, it's a case file that Ma'am had. She didn't give it back to me."

"Um, I don't remember any left on the desk, but you are welcome to have a look… Do you mind if I don't come and look with you? The baby is sat on the nerves in my legs. I have only just got comfy, and I really can't face moving again."

"Oh, Ok, sounds painful… It's fine, don't you worry. I won't be long. She may have left it in one of her drawers, anyway."

"Ah …they are locked, but I've got a master key somewhere…." Rooting around in her own desk drawer, Judy then produces a gold desk key.

"This is it! You'd never be able to imagine what we've found with this magic little key… The Professional

Standards lot they love it! Dubious DC's and the like, think that once they have locked it up in their desks that's it, it's safe! Let's hope Ma'am doesn't have any skeletons!" She says this with a laugh. I know that Judy thinks her words were a joke, but that's exactly what I'm hoping for. Not a skeleton as such, but just something that she might have thought was irrelevant...

I push open the heavy door and in I go. I feel so anxious. I know technically that I should not be doing this, but maybe, just maybe, I'll find something. As I enter, I realise how the smell of her office has changed. Normally there is the overpowering scent of Christian Dior's Poison. Her perfume. It's funny, I had not considered it before, but there was something quite animalistic about Ma'am Gordon. She definitely liked to leave her scent.

I'm not really sure what I'm looking for, but I put on a pair of search gloves anyway. I prefer to be over, rather than under cautious. There is nothing immediately obvious as to what I seek. Nothing appears to have been left out on the sides... In fact, I know that Ma'am wouldn't be remotely impressed. Montgomery is clearly not as tidy as she is. There are a number of half-drunk coffee cups left out, and the desk has papers scattered across it. I take a brief look, but it all appears to be resource planning information, and obviously of no use to me. I go over to the first desk drawer and I unlock it; my mouth goes dry as I look inside. Nothing, just hanging files, and most of them are empty.... I hear Judy outside. "Find what it was?" A little panicked because I don't want her coming in, I respond "Um, No... Not yet, I'll be done in a minute."

"Ok Hun, well, I've got to nip to the lav. Little bugger, he's now sat on my bladder... I'll try not to be long, but I can only waddle these days... Just pull the door to, and pop the key back on my desk when you are done."

I feel relieved at this. It gives me more time to look properly as I have just opened up the other desk drawer. It appears to be where Ma'am keeps her kit. Not much here, just her stab vest and an old-style 'Asp!' Blimey, she has had that some years! I go to close the drawer as nothing has immediately jumped out, but as I try to, something is in the way. I try again and see that it is an evidence bag. Pulling at it, I free it from the drawer mechanism so that it will close, and then I see that it has another bag inside. A carrier bag...... Jackpot! I have found it!

Josephine

I arrived at the library, early as usual, and I unlocked the big double frosted glass entrance doors. The musty smell of the books, and the stale air hits me. You would have thought that I would have gotten used to it over the years. But I am glad that I haven't, as it's not unpleasant, nor a smell that I mind. I actually find it quite homely. I feel safe here. I lock the doors again immediately behind me. It's nowhere near opening time yet. I then go over to logon to my computer. It is very slow in loading and I can see on my desk a number of notes, and memos that need my attention. I decide that I'll deal with them later on. I still feel a little fragile after last week. Today is my first day back in since it all happened and I really do need to get organised.

I sit there for a moment, collecting my thoughts, and then there is a bang at the door. I study the silhouette through the glass, and I can tell that it is Imogen, my boss.

"I didn't expect you in..." She says, as I open the door to her.

"That's why I'm in so early, to open up... Well... you look better than I thought...."

"Sorry, what? Why?"

"Well... after your attack. My sister told me."

"Um yes, my attack, how did she know?"

"Oh, she goes to your mum's church. She was telling them all at the coffee morning. It sounded horrific. Mind you, she said it happened after you left here... That can't be right though? .... Did you have a nice bit of holiday before... well ...? What exactly did happen?"

She has not even got her coat off, and she's firing questions at me. Questions, that I was not ready to answer. I was still in shock from it myself, but not for the reasons she would think. It was just too close for comfort. I had never once anticipated that I might get hurt in all of this. Well, not again.

I start telling a version of the events, and then I don't know what happens. I start to cry. Big heaving sobs. Tears begin cascading down my face. I even have big snot bubbles; I can't even speak.

"Oh, my goodness, Josephine, should you really be in? Look... Go home, you clearly need some time to get over this... "

I nod my head as I can't say another word. I didn't know it at the time, but I was crying because of HIM, and because of what he did to me. No one had asked me how I was. No one had taken care of me. No one had even believed me, and her little bit of concern had made it all come to the surface... Mum had refused to believe it, as in her mind, the rape didn't happen. Mum had convinced herself that I was a slut, who had been caught out by getting pregnant. I gratefully took up Imogen's offer, and I took the rest of the day off. I went home, and I spent much of the day sleeping. I was just so tired.

DS Rachel Cooper

I sent the knife that I had found, straight to forensics. Graham had wanted to know its provenance. He said something to me about budgetary constraints. Apparently, they have stopped just running knives that have been 'found' as a matter of course, unless it is obvious that it has actually been used in connection with a crime... It seems rather stupid to me, as how do you know either way, unless you run the thing through the system! Anyway, I made up some excuse about it being linked to a cold case that was in its infancy, so it had yet to be granted a budget.... He did the whole thing.... "As it's you, I'll authorise it this time, blah, blah, blah". He slightly annoys me. They all do when they are like this.... It's not as though it's a favour. It's still to do with a job, and it's not his money anyway. I never really understand why people make things so hard. Give them a little bit of power, and it goes straight to their head!

The other items that I had found in the carrier bag were also very interesting, and I really had no idea as to why Ma'am didn't just book them into evidence. I know that I need to tread carefully, as I shouldn't really have any of them. Ma'am must have had her reasons for not booking them in, but for now, I'm not sure what they were. There was also this letter; and from what I could establish, it was a full-on confession to the murder of Colin Joseph. At present, I do not know who the author is, but it appears to me, that they may be the biological mother of Shelley Jones. That letter and the carrier bag of stuff, has also given context to that polaroid that was found at Joneses home address. John, when I quizzed him over it before, had thought it had been left with Shelley when she was abandoned. So, it is all starting to make sense. Maybe Shelley really did have nothing to do with this?

Anyway, what I need now is for the knife to come back with some forensic link to this, or any other case, and to find out if John can help me with identifying who Shelley's biological mother actually is. I decide to strike whilst the iron is hot, so I make the call. Bugger! Straight to voicemail. I leave a message for him to ring me back, and then I get on with the work that I'm actually supposed to be doing today. I have got a meeting, with my DI later over my caseload, and to be honest, I've been so preoccupied with this, I've got absolutely nothing to show him.

Josephine

After that last time, I remained sensible, and I didn't seek any terminal justice for the far too many wronged victims. The vulnerable that the criminal justice system had simply let down. I knew now that I was not invincible. I was not the superhero that I had invented in my head. The 'Batgirl' of the paedophile world. I was no caped crusader, and I had no sidekick or butler to assist me in my quest. Instead, I kept my head down, and I decided to focus on my career at the library. Imogen was happy to support me both financially and emotionally (at times), and after many years of both working, and studying part-time, I managed to graduate with a Master's Degree in Library Science. I still remember just how proud my mum had been. It was shortly after then, that sadly Mum had gotten sick.

Cancer.

Josephine

That day was like any other. I had been to work, and then on to the gym. I had only started attending my local 'Fitness First', after my mum had passed on. I had no idea that she would have deteriorated quite so quickly, and so, I had only done it to help her on her way. Watching her in so much pain was horrendous. Helping her along, seemed to be the right thing to do…. Anyway, it was certainly no different to the peace that I had already given to the others.

I had started at the gym as a way of keeping myself occupied. After Mum, I was lost. Mum and I were never that close, but she was my mum, and now I was an orphan. Yes, I was in my 30's, and supposedly an adult, but it felt no less raw. My workplace had been good over it. Imogen was really wonderful; she had been very compassionate. I had been given all of the leave that I had needed, and she had even gotten her sister to help me out with the funeral arrangements. The service was just lovely, and everything Mum would have wanted. I had not been to the church for years as I could not shift the feeling, of having been failed by them.

Anyway, the Priest; Father John, he gave a moving sermon. It was clear that he had held Mum in very high regard. It had felt strange to me, as my mother had never shown me much kindness, or warmth. However, it was apparent that she had radiated these qualities through her work at the Church. The loss felt by her departure, was abundantly clear as there was not a dry eye amongst the other parishioners.

Anyhow, with Mum gone, I needed a distraction, and after I had completed all of my studies; the day-to-day humdrum of the library was simply not enough. Going to the gym, had been a somewhat radical addition to my other rather quiet life. I enjoyed the classes and the running machine. It gave me a boost that I never realised I needed.

This one day, however, I had just finished my weights class, and I was making my way back to the car. It was then that I saw HIM. A chill immediately hit my spine when I saw his white-blond hair and familiar physique. Although he was older, I was sure that it was definitely him. Feeling quite sick, my instant reaction was to run. The most basic of instincts had come over me… Fight or flight. I was unprepared and I felt vulnerable, so I hurried towards the car. However, once my initial panic had subsided, and I had reached its safety, it hit me. The anger that I still felt was so very strong. I ran back, no longer fearful. I wanted to confront him. I now knew exactly what he was. I got to the corner of the street where I'd seen him, and there he was, just ahead of me. I ran at him. Adrenaline pumping. I was going to get some answers, but as I am just within touching distance, he turns. It's not him. Embarrassed, I immediately apologised to this innocent man. I realise that it was never him. My mind was playing tricks. However real or not, seeing a ghost from my past, it had awoken something within me. I still needed answers.

Shelley

I was finally feeling that we might be getting somewhere. John had called me. He was meant to be coming in with the girls, but had cancelled me as he had received a call from Rachel. She had said she needed to discuss something with him urgently. Obviously, I told him "Yes, yes, go!" I would see him in a few days, maybe she had found something. Something that was to prove my innocence! I had a really good feeling!!

John

I made my way in, and straight to the Cold Cases Office. I was intrigued as to what she had found out. She was candid with me, but then she showed me a letter that she said she had 'discovered'. She refused to discuss its origin, or let me read it, but we both agreed that the handwriting was a match. It was the same as on the note that Shelley had received, and although clearly a much younger scribe, it was highly likely that it would have been the same person, who also wrote the text on the polaroid. The only part of the letter, that she would let me see was the author's sign-off. It appeared to be a jumble of numbers and letters. And had I not seen it before, I would have been puzzled, but as I had, I knew exactly what it was.

John

These days I didn't trust my own judgement. I had no idea what the letter actually contained, but I knew that it had to be significant enough for DS Cooper to have called me in to discuss it.

I made the call
"Larry Heart." The call echoed. It was clear that I was on loudspeaker...
"Hi Larry, it's John Jones."
"Hi John, yes I can see now, your name has just come up. Look I'm in the car, is it urgent?"
"Well, yes... everything to me is urgent if it gets Shelley acquitted!" I say this in a harsher tone than I meant, but he gets the message...
"Sorry, Mate, yes I know, it's just, I'm about to go into the Nick. I've got a drunk in charge. Young lad larking about and getting into an open car with his mates. He was pissed... but the car, it moved, and he's grabbed the

hand-break to stop it. Bloody probationer who needs a collar, he comes around the corner and catches him in the act. The silly bugger, he also made a significant statement at the scene; that he had touched the hand-break to stop it moving. So… he is bang to rights on a technicality... His dad is a mate from the golf club, so I said I would do all I can…."

"Yes right…. totally understand." Although actually all the while thinking, "like I give a shit about a poxy fine and points on your licence job, when Shelley is still locked up for a murder that she didn't commit!"

I'm just about managing to keep my cool. I tell him that he can call me back later, and just like that he is gone.

I'm frustrated at still not knowing what to do, so I call Shelley's mum to ask her to pick up the girls. I then go for a run. I needed to clear my head.

DS Rachel Cooper

What I have here is a confession. It is clear that they have intimate knowledge of the crime, and they have provided the physical evidence, which we never had before. I just don't understand why Ma'am never did anything with it. She's usually so thorough, a dog with a bone. She said it herself, she likes results. Crimes detected and the accused accountable. I have tried calling her, but she has not picked up, and to be honest, it is not really a conversation that I'm relishing... "Oh, Hi Ma'am... Yes, well whilst I was snooping in your office, I found a couple of things that don't make any sense..." My god, she'd have me on garden leave before I'd even finished my sentence. Maybe it was a godsend that she was currently unavailable. It gives me the time to come up with a different angle.

John also definitely knew something about that letter. I could see it in his eyes, but I suppose it's like a game of poker at the moment. We both have a hand, but neither are sure of the other's motives. Is this all an elaborate plan on his part, to get his guilty wife off? I'll wait for the lab results to come back on the knife first, and then I'll work out my next move.

DI Smart has also been wanting a 1-to-1. Apparently, the powers that be are looking at ways to trim costs, and they have our department in their sights. He needs to showcase our recent achievements to keep us funded! ... Ha, what recent achievements? I have been so occupied with a case that isn't even a case, I have got nothing else done. I'll have to see if there is a quick win that I can pull out of the bag, and pronto!

Shelley

So, about four months ago, I was contacted by a student at one of the London Universities. She was doing a Doctorate on the Psychology and the Treatment of Women in Prisons, with a particular focus on suicide attempts. She had used a freedom of information request, and that had identified that HMP Lightbridge had had a higher rate of attempted (and unfortunately successful) suicides, than any other women-only prison. Therefore, she had wanted to profile me in her research. We had had a few meetings over the months, with the agreement of both my support team and the Governor. Everyone agreed that it was a good thing that someone external was looking into this worrying trend.

Emily Joyce was her name, and she appeared very professional. A petite girl in her late twenties. Blonde hair always tied up in a bun, smart trouser-suits, and with her black-rimmed glasses, she looked very much the part.

The unit staff had permitted the numerous interviews to take place in one of the side rooms. It had allowed our sessions to take place in an as relaxing environment as possible. Soft chairs, natural light, etc, etc. The Governor too was happy that there was a spotlight on Lightbridge. She felt that too many of us were failed there. The lucky few like me who survived, were brought here for her, and her team to put back together.

Anyway, Emily asked me lots of questions surrounding prison life. Questions concerning both my physical and mental care, and what I thought had led me to try and take my own life. She also had me complete so many questionnaires. I couldn't quite see the relevance of some of them, but it was nice to be occupied and not always absorbed in my own thoughts. I remember when she first told me that I would not be named in her paper, but known only as subject 007. This had made me smile, as I had always fancied being a Bond-girl!

Over the weeks and months, we had built up quite a rapport. I liked her. In the last session, however, she turned to me, and asked if I would mind chatting about why I was in prison in the first place? She wanted to know about my case. I told her the abridged version, and she had seemed really interested in what had happened to me. She then advised that if I was agreeable, she would like to write about me from a non-scientific perspective, in her on-line blog. Initially, I didn't know what to say. I told her that there wasn't much more to tell her, and certainly not enough for a blog; as the truth was, I didn't do it. She said that she had really gotten to know me over the months, and she believed me. She also said her readers would find my account fascinating. She really wanted to tell my story.

I obviously said that I needed to discuss it with John, but in principle, her blogging about my experience didn't seem a bad idea, and if he and the Governor were agreeable; why not! She told me that her blog was called the 'Inside Story'. She had written about many of her other research subjects. She also said that she had quite an online following.

So, yesterday was my first blog interview. I started at the very beginning. I had left the details of my conception out. It didn't feel right me telling the world that my mother had been raped. However, I did speak about being a foundling, and of the adoption, and how supportive my parents were back then, and still continued to be today. I gave a potted history of my education, my DNA Research, and how that had led me to work for the police. I wanted to describe Jo as the ogre that she had become in my head, but I knew it wouldn't help my cause.... I then went on to explain that on one very ordinary September day, I went to process a crime scene where a body had been found. I advised how I had thought nothing of it, and then through purely circumstantial evidence, and that I still wasn't sure how it happened, I ended up being charged for the murder. I was convicted of killing a man that I had never met, and had had no dealings with, bar process his remains post mortem. My only link was that I shared familial DNA, which suggested that we were related. In fact, it was highly likely that he was my biological father. One day, I was a wife, a mother, and a respected Forensic Scientist, who had helped put criminals away, and the next I had been convicted, made restricted status, and placed in a closed prison. She took a copious number of notes.

She asked me if I wanted to share that I'd tried to take my own life. It didn't really bother me if the outside world were made aware, of just how desperate prison life was, so I gave her the go-ahead to include it in whatever she put together. She said she would write it up that night, and send it through to me via the Governor's email. She wanted to be as transparent as possible, and said that if any of us had any objections to what was written, they could be ironed out before she uploaded it for the world to see. Anyway, she kept her word, and right now I have a printed version of the 'Inside Story' before me. The Governor had been emailed it. She had printed it off, and a member of staff brought it into me. After reading it I was amazed at the emotion that she'd managed to capture, and just how much of a soap opera my life had become. It was a good read, it was just such a shame that the events that it detailed were true, and not just a story of fiction, conjured up from someone's head.

The Governor thought it was well written, and she had raised no objections for it to go online. There was no finger-pointing over the suicide attempt. She'd kept that factual, and anything else just documented my history to date. The Governor responded on my behalf and that was that. My 'Inside Story' was uploaded to the World Wide Web.

It was nothing new to me having my name out there on the internet. My research papers and journals had been out there for years, and of course, there was the mainly biased coverage from my trial, but this was different. This was something that I had control over. Believe me, it's not often you have hold of the reins whilst being locked up. In here and HMP Lightbridge, practically every decision is made for you. From the time you get up, and up until the time you go to bed. This was new, this was a luxury and it felt great.

Josephine

I didn't know what I expected to find. I opened Google, and I looked at the vacant search field…. I didn't actually know his name, well, not his official name anyway, but I just wanted to see, if I could find anything out. I typed in "CJ Engineer" and I got results. However, not the ones I wanted. An Engineering Company in Bolton, and a Publishing House in Thetford, but neither were of any use to me. I then tried "CJ Mechanical Engineer, Middle East" but that was fruitless too. Endless job-advert listings. Having seen him, or who I thought was him, it had made me desperate for answers. I'm not sure if I wanted revenge, or what it was, I just wanted to see if I could find him. Deleting the search field, I tried one more go. "CJ paedophile." As silly as it seemed, I knew he'd never advertise himself as such, but maybe he'd done it before, and or then did it again? I might have been in a long line of victims, and one of those may have already got justice; had closure. A court case that I had missed, a news-article, anything... What I actually found however really surprised me.... And I don't know how I had not known about it before. There were people out there, just like me. I don't mean victims. There were plenty of those. No, I meant hunters. They did what I did, well ... without the finality. They exposed these monsters safely, and faceless, and from behind a computer screen. It seemed the perfect way to continue my work.

John

Jackie has come up trumps, and I don't know how, or where she found it, but she did. She had left me a voicemail to say that she had found the missing part of the letter, and that she had forwarded it on to Shelley at the Unit. Her voicemail was cryptic. "Hi John, look, I've been given that missing part of the letter that you were looking for. I'm forwarding it on to Shelley… but it's very interesting reading! I really hope it helps." I wasn't sure what she meant, and I really wished she had sent it straight on to me, but I understood that rightfully, it was Shelley's. I would just have to be patient; I would just have to wait to see it.

Shelley

My post was handed to me that afternoon, and straight away I saw the HMP header. I hurriedly opened up the crisp white envelope. John still hadn't told me the outcome of the meeting with DS Cooper, but maybe, just maybe things had progressed quicker than even he knew. I was instantly in shock. Is this really happening? I could not believe what I was reading. Rather than the elation that I had anticipated, it was the absolute reverse.

THEY WERE SENDING ME BACK.

Apparently, I had been cleared by the medical team, my therapists, key workers, support workers, and the Governor. You name it, each and every one of them had cleared me as fit to return to the Prison. As before, I was to remain classified as 'restricted status' and returned to the closed prison. They cited that this was for my own safety due to my links with the police, and because I had shown absolutely no remorse, or acceptance of my crime. I had an instant regret over that blog. I should never have said anything... and rather than it aiding my release, as I had hoped, it had put another nail into my coffin. I crumbled to the floor; my head was pounding. I was unable to catch my breath. It's over, I am going to end up dying in that place. This had been the cruellest of interludes.

Consumed by dread and anger at how unfair it all was, I begin almost subconsciously to smash up my room. Lashing out, my arms and legs are flailing, I punch and kick out at the furniture. It was like I was possessed. In the process, I manage to cut my arms and forehead. My blood is everywhere, and I'm also sweating and crying. I've got every emotion racing through me. I have never been so out of control. At that very moment, a member of staff must have looked in on me, and they have hit the alarm.   I don't remember anymore after that, as I'm sat on and sedated.

John

For God's sake! It's like she has a bloody self-destruct button! She had a great little job at the university, but no, she takes that bloody job with Jo. We are managing with her in segregation. We were working on her appeal, but she tries to top herself.   She is then doing really well at the unit, she is looking more like herself, and now I'm told that she has kicked off, and has had to be sedated. What the actual fuck? Every time that everything is on an even keel, she does something to sabotage it. I'm doing my best here, but I need a bloody break!

I was called by the staff to tell me that the visit for today, was cancelled. They said Shelley was not in a good state physically or mentally, so we'd have to arrange for another time. I understood, of course, I did, but I was desperate. Desperate to know if the internal mail from Jackie, had reached her yet. I just hoped it wasn't that, which had set her off today.

I cancelled her mum from picking up the girls. I didn't need her help today. I just needed to be a normal dad. I need them more than they need me at the moment. I get to the school gate, just in time to see their smiling little faces. "Daddy!" They shout as they are released. Running toward me like whippets at the racetrack. I bend down and I take both of them into my arms. They are warm, and they have such a comforting scent. I'm so exhausted with it all. I want to cry, but instead I take a deep breath and say... "Right then! Who wants pizza?"

Josephine

I had learnt from the last time, just how close I had come to being seriously hurt, or even worse caught in the act. I had no remorse over my actions, I was just delivering a little justice. Doing what others had failed at. And as I couldn't find HIM, giving another some closure, was in my mind the next best thing. My calling however, was one to be handled with caution. I knew that. Times had changed since I had first started out. The science was getting more and more sophisticated; DNA techniques had advanced and 'Big Brother' saw our every move. I had also matured, and the risk versus reward was too much. These days, not only did our physical footsteps leave a trace, we also left them online. When I think back to the old modem warbling away when I was trying to get on the internet, and just how slow it was; that had only been a decade, or so ago... and now we had smartphones. A little computer with instant access to the web, available immediately in our handbag or back pocket. This little bit of technology, however handy it was, it also meant that our every move was easily tracked. I knew that I had to be careful. Previously, I had been a lone wolf. I had only had myself to worry about. This new potential avenue, meant that I would be part of the pack. The groups; I had learnt were very successful in trapping these creatures, but their methods meant that they actively communicated with the police. Creating a relationship and passing on the evidence that they had collated. Some of them were seen as vigilantes, causing more harm than good. I had personally felt more closely aligned to these types. Taking the law into their own hands. Outing them and delivering the odd kicking. It was only what these vile individuals had deserved. Others, however, they compiled case files of each vulgar interaction. The problem however, with both of these methods; was that you made yourself known to the authorities…. And therefore, after much research, it all seemed too risky. I had no interest in putting my existence on any police forces database, so I did what I never thought I could do….

I let it go.

I decided that now was the time that I needed to start living, and I began doing just that by selling Mum and Dad's house, and by moving on.

Shelley

I can't stop crying. I feel so ashamed of how I acted. Rage had overtaken me, and I had been totally out of control. I look like I have been in a fight, and I definitely know, that my opponent was left without a scratch. None of it served a purpose, I am still going back. I have not even seen John. He was told to stay away. I suppose it's their way of ensuring that they don't reward bad behaviour. My privileges, my visits - they have been removed.

The Governor, she came to see me personally, and she reminded me of why I was in their care in the first place, and what sentence I was serving. "Michelle, acting up won't stop me from sending you back. You've been assessed as fit, and as such you will serve the rest of your sentence back at the Prison. Don't think for one second that your little paddy yesterday, will make me keep you here". I could see the disappointment that she had in me. Did she not read that blog? I didn't do it. How can she think I had a paddy out of what? Petulance? I made my apologies, but I knew it had fallen once again on deaf ears. I had no way out. My fate once again was sealed.

DS Rachel Cooper

I bit the bullet and I took what I had to DI Smart. He agreed with me, that there appeared to be a linked series. Granted there were two convictions, Michelle Jones and the wife of one of the other victims, but it was just too big a coincidence. I also showed him the "new evidence" that I had found in Ma'am's Office. This was what really piqued his interest. I showed him the confession, and I explained to him that I had spoken to Michelle's Husband John, just to get clarity on the photo and the handwriting. He was OK with that, and thankfully he confirmed that I had not breached anything that could potentially have undermined the investigation. "Well… he's still a serving officer. He is still one of the good guys!" I was massively relieved. I think that if I had been talking to Ma'am, she would have gone ballistic, and would have had my warrant card by now.

Anyway, I'm still waiting on the lab report on the knife. I chased it up the other day, but they have a backlog, and as mine's not a live investigation, it is at the back of the queue... Typical!

John

Larry never called me back, but it doesn't matter. I've got it. The "Enclosed" and it tells me everything that I need to know.

It had been two weeks since Shelley's outburst. Two weeks since I had actually spoken to her. We had a visit today, and she was in a bad way; tears were just tumbling down her face. It is heart-breaking to see someone that you love, so broken, and in such despair. What is worse however, is seeing that, and knowing that there is nothing that I could do.

She hadn't looked at any other of her post, not since receiving the official transfer notification. She had not been able to concentrate, and had lost interest in everything. She is barely eating, and she is only drinking due to her sheer dehydration, which is a result of her non-stop crying. It all makes sense now. The outburst, her self-destruction. She had nowhere else to go.

Anyway, I have it now and I'm going to trace her and make her hand herself in. The official channels have had long enough. I am going to sort this mess out myself.

DS Rachel Cooper

My god, he is really good at his job, and he is really going to go to town on this one. What was once solely my hunch, has now been confirmed, and the DI is determined to right a wrong. I can't tell John. This all has to stay in-house, but I know that he will soon have his wish, and his family will be back together.

She will be held accountable.

I also know, what all of this has done to Shelley. I've seen it first hand, and for my involvement in that, I will forever be sorry.

John

My hands are shaking, and my heart pounding. I have never ever operated outside of the law, and I have never done anything for my own gain, but I truly believe that this is the only way. I press enter on the keyboard and it is done!

She is now circulated on the Police National Computer. She is now officially WANTED.

Josephine - Present day.

I had no choice. I had to come back. I had had no idea that she had not been released. I was so convinced that what I had handed into the police, it would have made her conviction unsafe. Why did no one act?

After that day I went straight to the airport. I knew I needed to get away. Be out of the country, before they worked out who I was, and how to find me. Of course, I didn't make the obvious flight, so I decided upon Thailand. I wanted to lie-low for a bit and to have some time to think. I don't even remember the flight, as I must have slept for the majority of it. I was just so exhausted with it all. I do remember being woken for the inflight meals, but after that, nothing. It was actually one of the easiest of flights that I had ever taken, and considering it was six times the length of a flight to Spain, I had done really well. Sleep was clearly the way to go on long-haul!

Bangkok was hot and humid. I had decided that I would stay there for a couple of days, and then I would really start my search. For the first time ever, I finally knew his full name; it was "Charlie Jacobs". He may have cashed-in on his sob story in the newspaper article, but that was the last time he'd pretend to be a victim. I would make sure of it.

That first night was surreal, I had checked into a city hotel. I had plenty of money, so I had chosen a nice looking one. Marble flooring, a pianist in the lobby. I had even booked a double room. I decided that I would explore my surroundings before I got on with my pursuit, and I found that the place was amazing. I couldn't believe it, but I actually saw a working elephant in the middle of the city street, it was mad!

Anyway, I think it was the second day, it was really hot, and I had gone out to find somewhere to eat. I had recognised a male; he was from the same inbound flight as I had been on. He had his arms linked with a petite young girl, and he was just about to stroll into, what was no mistaking, a brothel. He must have been at least three times her age. The sight of it instantly put my back up, but I knew that I had to stay focused. Time was not on my side; I couldn't be getting sidetracked. I knew that they would be searching for me.

DS Rachel Cooper

It's official. She is down as a named suspect. I typed it into the system myself. It felt wrong initially, but you can't let these things go. Justice has to be served. It's not for us to decide who is innocent or guilty.

Josephine

So, months and months passed, and I had finally found HIM. I had become a dab-hand at open-source research. I had had no idea how common his name was, nor just how many engineers globally, that shared it. Even using a location as a means to narrow down the search, it had meant that I still had to trawl profile after profile. Linked-in, industry journals, company websites. I needed to be sure.

Then, one sunny afternoon, after a morning of swimming, I had gone into the Internet cafe, (I still thought it was too risky to have a phone) and I found HIM.

He was staring back at me. Those cold blue eyes.

He had got himself a promotion, and was working on a multimillion-dollar HVAC installation. As I read the screen, the words meant nothing to me - HVAC?? He was however, clearly very successful. I had not left any mark on his life, unlike the stain he had left on mine, or on hers for that matter. He was oblivious to it all. I had done all of this to protect her, but I had failed. It was time to right the wrong.

I had lost count of the number of times that I typed her name into Google. The number of journals and research papers that she'd once been "famous" for, were now dwarfed by the tabloid reports, detailing her murderous ways. "Cold Killer", "Inside Job" I refused to read on. I knew her destruction was down to me. I just needed this little bit of closure. I needed HIM gone for both of our sakes.

DS Rachel Cooper

It is done, all of our ducks are in a line. I have made sure that we have everything. Exhibits, Witness Statements, Forensic Reports. There is no room for error on this one, and there is absolutely no chance of her denying it. I am also riding shotgun again. The Boss is the Senior Investigating Officer. I totally respect that this has to be done properly, and they are as experienced as they come. We have also got the OK from Senior Management. We know that she is travelling back today, and Uniform are going to arrest her later tonight.

John

I got the call; I still have some mates in the know that are willing to help me out. She is coming into Heathrow. British Airways flight, EK 9943, arrival time 22:50 hours, terminal 2.

I am on my way there now.

Superintendent Jo Gordon

I have had a wonderful time away. I had no idea how the sharing of ideas and my best practice would make me feel. This is my calling. No politics, just the ability to demonstrate how things should be done. I have a renewed focus. Montgomery, I'm sure will have done his best, but there is important work to be done, and I'm the only girl for the job.

Josephine

I was so close. I had arrived four weeks before, and I could not believe how different Dubai was to anywhere else that I had ever been. I had felt immediately uncomfortable there. I wasn't sure if that was because of the relentless humidity, or the fact that I was within touching distance of HIM.

It was a very busy city, and at night it reminded me of the 'Oxford Street Christmas Lights'. Everywhere seemed to sparkle.

I had tracked down his office, and I had watched him come and go on a number of occasions, but he was never alone. He seemed to have a Protection Team. Did he know that I was after him? Or had he other enemies? Either way, I knew that it would be difficult to get close to him. I knew my time would come, I just needed to be patient.

Anyway, I was having one of my "patient" days at the Kite Beach. I was chilling out, and catching some rays…. In fact, after the initial culture shock, I had actually started to like it over there. I had never been somewhere so busy, so bright, so man-made. Construction loomed over you wherever you went. I was enjoying it whilst I could, as I knew that this would soon be over. I had absolutely no doubt, that once I'd done what I was planning, that would be it for me. One thing I was sure of, was that the laws in the United Arab Emirates were not to be broken lightly. Capital punishment enacted by firing squad, stoning, or hanging was likely to be the finality that would set me free.

Josephine

In an absolute panic, I booked myself on to the first flight out of there. I remember running into the booking hall. To an outsider I would have looked desperate, and I was. I needed to get home to her. She was like a caged bird, and only I could open the door.

I had been killing time, and I had idly been surfing the net, when I thought I would google her. The usual stuff had come up; her journals – filling me every time with pride, but then something else caught my eye.

This was new. A blog. A blog about my daughter.

It was called the 'Inside Story', and it was a raw depiction of where she had come from (minus the rape, of course) and it detailed everything that she had been through. Then I saw it, and I felt instantly sick. She had tried to kill herself.

John

I had checked my watch, and her flight was due in now. As I approached the terminal, I was on high alert. Adrenaline was pumping throughout my body; I had an end in sight. I still can't believe that she had a PNC record. I think it must have been fate that she had previously been reported missing. Half of the work had already been done... The record was there, I just needed to add the wanted flag.

I had realised all of this as soon as I had deciphered her sign-off. I had immediately run her through the system as I had everything that I needed. Name, address, and date of birth. They had this all along, and it really didn't take a genius to break the code. After all, Shelley had cracked it when she was just a teenager! This was typical of Jo. She had her detection, her clear up and as far as she was concerned, it was over. Well, it will never be over for her. I'll see to that!

I have two-toned it for the last five miles. I wanted to be there at the point of her arrest. I really didn't need any questions being asked over the pony offence that I had circulated her for. I had used a drug supply job in order to flag her as wanted. The missing person's marker would have been enough to speak to her, and to check on her welfare, but I couldn't risk losing her, not again. It had to be done this way, I knew that Shelley couldn't hold out much longer. Her incarceration was literally killing her.

I dumped the car in the valet parking, and ran in. I didn't want anyone pulling up the crime report, and realising that she had absolutely nothing to do with it. Time was not on my side.

My mobile begins to ring. It's George, my mate from Training School.

"John, my old mucker... Are you here yet, Mate? ....
We've got her."

I breathe a sigh of relief.

"Just arrived, Mate. I'm on my way." I begin to run, and I become a little short of breath as I purposefully navigate my way in.

Superintendent Jo Gordon

It's been a long fucking night. In fact, it's safe to say, that this had been one of my worst. The interview was long. It seemed like an ambush. After every question "No comment." Well, there really was nothing to say. What explanation is there? It was a mistake! An error in judgement! Time had passed slowly whilst I had waited for the CPS to make their decision, and I was finally at the Custody Desk. Bastard Bob is there, as I've taken to calling him. He is such a smug little fucker. I outrank him and I always will. He will never really amount to anything. He's too fat and lazy.

"Well then Ma'am…" Bob says with a really broad smile across his face. "Shall we get on with it?"
Rachel is to the side of me, as is Kevin Smart.
Bob starts with his well-rehearsed spiel. He has said this a countless number of times, but I can see that he has never enjoyed it as much as he is doing so right now.

"Right then, so the CPS have been consulted and they have granted the following charges. However, before we get on to that, please can you confirm your full name, address, and date of birth."

"Jo, um... I mean Josephine Patricia Gordon... 01/10/1979. 59 South Quay, London, SE9 4JD"

"Ok then, "Josephine", you are being charged with two counts. One, that between 21st March 2019 and 12th January 2020, you perverted the course of justice; namely, that you tampered with evidence. A knife that had been handed to police. It is believed that you wiped it clean with a police specific wipe, with the intention of eliminating any evidence, that posed doubt over the conviction of Mrs Michelle Jones. You also failed to enter into evidence, or further investigate a signed confession to the murder of Colin Joseph...."

"You are also charged with gross misconduct in a public office, in particular in relation to your statutory duty of disclosure under the Criminal Procedures and

Disclosures Act 1996. In particular section 7a and paragraph 72 of the Attorney General's Guidelines on disclosure, namely you were aware of material, that showed that a conviction was unsafe. However, you failed to disclose this new evidence to the CPS, or to the Defence Team of Mrs Michelle Jones...."

Bob takes a deep breath and continues...

"You do not have to say anything, but it may harm your defence if you do not mention now, something which you later rely on in court. Anything you do say may be given in evidence."

Bob smiles at me, but I've not heard a word of it. I make no reply. I can't.

"Right then, if you can just sign your autograph there..." Bob thrusts the electronic scribe into my hand, and directs me to sign on the pad, acknowledging what he has just said. He then gets Rachel to do the same... "Rachel, are you the Charging Officer? If so, pop your paw print there...yes, that's it. Lovely."

It is a process, that I have been integral to countless times, but never in a million years did I think that I would be the one being charged. How did I get here? I have given this job everything, and I mean everything!

"Right then, any issues over bail?" says Bob.
Rachel is clearly embarrassed, and bows her head and so Kevin chirps in.
"No, we will not remand. We obviously need her warrant card. Just bail her for her first appearance at court."
"Righty-ho, that's all done and dusted... Billy!" Bob shouts this from across his shoulder. "Nip into Prisoner's Property (Store), will you? Get number 9 her personal, will you?"

Billy hurries off, and then he returns, dumping the bag that contains my possessions on the desk.

"Right then, everything is returned, bar your warrant card... sign here... Right young lady, you are free to leave." I look over at the wall of faces to my right. My colleagues, no not colleagues, my subordinates. I cannot believe that they have done this to me!

"Ah yes! Don't forget your paperwork. You mustn't forget your first appearance." Bob tells me this, practically singing it. I look through him. I won't give him the satisfaction of making eye-contact.

"Show this one out Bill, she's done for in here."

And that was it. I'm escorted out of the building, and into the cold mist of the early morning. I'm lost and I'm completely numb.

Josephine

I didn't sleep a wink on the flight. I had an awful feeling that something bad was about to happen, and I was desperate to get back, so that I could stop whatever it was. In fact, If I could have flown that plane myself, I would have done. I would have done anything, if it meant that I had got back sooner.

***

We land, and I could tell that something was going on. There was lots of chatter at the front of the cabin, and there was a delay in getting us off. The front doors are opened, and a number of police officers, all carrying guns pile on. I knew it! I'm on a flight with a load of terrorists! I look around to see if I can spot whoever it is, but as I turn my head, I realise that I am facing one of the armed officers' groins.

"Josephine Gilling?" I look up and nod.

".... I'm arresting you for the possession of cocaine with intent to supply. You do not have to say anything, but it may harm your defence, if you do not mention when questioned, something which you later rely on in court, and anything you do say may be given in evidence. Your arrest is necessary for you to be interviewed on tape and to prevent your further disappearance."

In shock I reply... "What? Cocaine? No .... What? That has to be a mistake? If it's in my bag, someone has planted it!"

"No mistake Madam, just come with us. You'll have your chance to have your say..."

I'm taken aback, but on autopilot, I do leave my seat. I'm flanked by two male officers, as I'm escorted off the plane and down through a number of breeze block constructed tunnels. I am then put into a side holding room. I'm not handcuffed, but I am patted down and my handbag, and coat are taken away from me. The room is sterile. It's painted white, with a fluorescent strip light above. There is an officer stood on the other side of the door, they are watching me. I can actually feel the intensity of their stare as they look through the transparent toughened glass. I then see hurried movement outside. I instantly recognise this athletic-looking man. He is my son-in-law.

John

I get through security; I flash my ID and I'm in. I walk straight over to George.

"Thanks for that Mate, we couldn't lose this one..."
"No problem, Mate, happy to oblige. Are you booking her in?"
"Um... no actually, I know it's not strictly PACE compliant..." I say slightly grimacing... "but I'm going to run her back to Central."
"Yeah, no problem. Our custody isn't open anyway, so I don't think you'll have a problem... Some little bastard had a dirty protest earlier and we're still waiting on the deep clean. He did an amazing job, if you know what I mean!"

... George and I have a laugh at this. It's weird just how desensitised over the years that you become.... And what the general public would find really rather repulsive, becomes actually quite amusing!

"Right, she's not been properly searched, just patted down. I can get Julie to give her a proper one before you take her."

"Yeah, thanks Mate, that would be great. Can you get the transfer docket and I'll be on my way?"

"No need Mate, she was never officially here. There is also a Misper marker that needs cancelling when you get her back. I've already done the wanted one, for the drugs...." He takes a breath.

"Julie, love, give her a proper search before John takes her, will you?"

"Yes, ok Sarge, let me just get my gloves."

This petite brunette officer, not too dissimilar in her physique to Shelley, slips past me to search my prisoner.

After a few minutes, and we are then on our way. I've cuffed her in a rear stack, and I'm walking her through the back of the police holding area, and out to my car, which has already been moved around the back, by another of George's helpful officers. He's even loaded her personal property into the car, so I have everything that I need. She hasn't said a word to me, nor I to her, bar me saying "Right. No silly business. I think you know why you're here. We need to get things sorted."

I place her in the rear of the vehicle, I'm taking a big risk, as I'd never normally transport a prisoner in this way, but I have no choice. I don't want a chaperone. I don't want anyone else involved in this. I've made sure she's strapped in, and that the child locks are on. I turn the key in the ignition and we're away.

Josephine

The air in the car is flat. It is dark outside, and I can see spots of rain appearing on the windscreen. The wipers kick in suddenly, making me jump. I can see John looking in his rear-view mirror at me. To and fro, to and fro. At the road, and then back again at me. I suppose in his mind, we were of equal danger. I needed him to know that I really did come in peace. I wanted to make things right. I clear my voice and go to speak...

"You're my Michelle's husband, aren't you?"
This appears initially to have taken him aback.
"How do you know?" He questions me.
"I've seen you at the house, and at the court case."
His back straightens.
"What, so you've been watching me?"
"Oh god no, not watching as such, I've just seen you, that's all."

"Ok …if that's all? Whatever that is supposed to mean. What do you mean by your Michelle? I take it that you are her biological mother then?"

"Yes, that's right."

"Well, to be honest, you look so similar, that it would be hard to believe that you were anyone else." Silence falls between us, and then I say…

"Can I ask? Am I really arrested for cocaine?"

John appears a little uneasy, and he shifts in his seat.

"Um, no, but I needed to catch up with you… Look. You are de-arrested, but I still need you to come into the Station."

"Is that to hand myself in? Because if it is? That is why I came back."

"Really?" I can hear the sarcasm in his voice.

"Yes!" I try to say this as earnestly as I can.

"Look, as soon as she was convicted, I went to the police. I gave them the evidence. I got them to give it straight to the Officer in Charge. The young lad, he promised me."

"Yes, but you didn't stay! You didn't take her place and make sure that something was done…" John then continues… "From what I can see, you skipped off on bloody holiday…" *Anger begins to rise in his voice.* "You left her to bloody rot!! You have destroyed her, US!"

The tension in the car is high, and I am trapped, I know I am. I'm handcuffed, and in the rear of the car with the doors locked. I want to do the right thing, but I have begun to panic. My head is pounding and I am sweating. The lights of the other cars are whizzing past us, as we speed down the motorway. I'm deep breathing, and I think I'm going to be sick. I start to wretch…

John looks back at me in the mirror. "Shit! Are you ok? What's happening?"
I manage to mouth "Panic attack."

He obviously believes me, because he takes the next lay-by, and we have come to a stop. The windows at the front of the car are opened, and I can feel the cold wet breeze on my face. I immediately start to feel better. Less clammy and more in control.

"Look, I'm sorry, I didn't mean to frighten you, or whatever it was that caused..." *He doesn't finish the first part of his sentence...* "But I just need you to tell the truth, and to get Shelley out".
I look up and nod. "Shelley? Is that what you call her?"
"Shit! I'm doing this all wrong, I shouldn't even be involved in this. I should have arrested you, and cautioned you by now, but I really need answers."

It's like he was thinking out loud. I'm not sure if he wants a response, so I stay quiet. I feel a bit better now, as John has given me a drink of water. He'd held a bottle of mineral water to my mouth, and I had guzzled it down.

"Right, are we ready to go?"

"Yes ready …. Look, I am going to do the right thing."

He straps me back in and he helps me get as comfortable as I can, and just like that we are away again.

John

The hour and a half had passed so quickly, even with the inevitable bottlenecks, that always occurred on the M25, and I finally felt like I was getting somewhere.

Shelley's mother is actually OK for a cold-blooded killer. It is funny how what would normally be black and white to me, has turned into grey. I am no longer the outsider in all of this. She told me everything. Not under caution, not as a police officer, but as her daughter's husband.

She had had such a traumatic life, but not that she saw it that way. They were just a set of circumstances that had shaped her, and skewed her perception of what was right and wrong. She actually needed my help rather than my judgement. I believed her when she said she had come back to save Shelley. Therefore, I didn't accompany her into the Front Office at the Central

Police Station. After I had gotten her out of the car, and I had removed the cuffs, I let her walk in alone to hand herself in. I knew that I needed to distance myself, if I was ever going to be able to stay in the Force. The rest was up to her. They had to believe her, and then acquit and set Shelley free. It was her only chance.

Josephine

I wasn't scared or anxious. In fact, I realised that I had actually been scared for most of my adult life. However, right here, and right now, I felt very much at peace.

There was another young officer at the desk. He couldn't have been much older than eighteen, so when I said that I wanted to confess to a murder, I think it was fear, that flashed initially across his face and then confusion. He was no longer playing dress-up. This was for real.

"Um…Right, ok…. so…." He was clearly stalling, whilst working out what to do… "Look, come in here." He opens up what I presume is an interview room. "I've just got to get someone. You stay there, I'll be back in a minute". I hear the door click as it shuts behind him. I am alone, and I take a seat on one of the blue cloth-covered chairs. Then I hear muffled radio chatter between the officer, and whoever he's taking guidance from.   Then suddenly the door swings open. It's the same officer. "Right ok, you sit tight. I have got someone from CID coming down.   They won't be long."

He looked so unsettled, and I'm not really sure what the delay is to be honest. They haven't even asked me who I've murdered. I thought that I would have been put straight into a cell, just like you see on the television, but so far, I've been invited to sit in a none too unpleasant room. I wait patiently. I half keep expecting him to pop his head around the door, and to ask if I want a cup of tea and a biscuit. It has all been rather civilised.

After about ten minutes, a harassed middle-aged woman comes in. Her hair is all over the place. I immediately notice her really ill-fitting trouser suit, with a less than white blouse underneath.

"Right ...so you've come to confess to a murder... have you?" I nod my head.

"Well, let's have it then... I suppose I should caution you. Do it properly."

She reels off the caution telling me I'm free to leave at any time... Really? I thought I would be locked up for sure.

"So, who is it that you've killed?" She asks me sarcastically...

Oh my god, she thinks I'm a crack-pot, she thinks I've made it all up... I start speaking as calmly as I can.... so, to demonstrate to her, that I'm not!

"My name is Josephine Gilling, and on 25th April 2018, I met a man called Colin Joseph at Bramley Wood, and I stabbed him to death and then I burnt the body. You have convicted Michelle Jones for this, but she didn't do it. I did. I am truly sorry."

"Right ok, well.... I wasn't expecting that" .... She pauses momentarily and then continues... "Well then "Josephine" let's get you through to Custody. It is rather serious what you have just told me, so we have a protocol to follow... So, based on what you have just said, I'm arresting you for the murder and unlawful disposal of Mr Joseph in April? Is that what you said?"

"Yes... Colin Joseph, 25th of April 2018..."

"So, you are arrested for the murder and unlawful disposal of "Colin Joseph" .... (she emphasises his name) on the 25th of April, at Bramley Wood. You do not have to say anything, but it may harm your defence if you do not mention when questioned, something which you later rely on in court, and anything you do say may be given in evidence."

"Ok" ... I reply.

"Ok..." she responds. "I just need to search you before going through. Have you anything on you, that can injure you, or me?"

"No nothing," I reply.

"Ok, then stand up. Let's get this done. Leave your coat and bag."

She pats me down, similar to what happened to me at the airport.

"Ok then." She says, and then on her radio that she has pulled out of her inside jacket pocket. (I note how much better the jacket now fits...)

"Custody receiving?"

"Yep... go ahead."

"Space for one female, please."

"Ok yes, what's it for and your ETA please?"

"30 seconds tops, we are in the Front Office. It's for Murder." There is a brief delay at the other end.

"Ok, Sarge says bring her through."

John

I'm desperate to know what's happening. I had parked right outside the Nick, I watched her go in, and then nothing. I had been pleased that she didn't run straight past me, but to be honest, I didn't think she would. I believed her when she said that she wanted to do the right thing. I sit there for a moment, and I notice that my breath has begun to steam up the car. I wipe away the condensation to make sure that I still have visibility, and after about 30 minutes, and when I'm sure that she will be in Custody, I call Larry.

Although it is late, he picks up immediately.

"John! Hi Mate, I'm so sorry I never came back to you. Did you get whatever it was sorted?"

"Look, things have moved on. The police have arrested the killer of Colin Joseph. It is a long story, but can you come to Central? I think she will need your help. It's Shelley's mum."

"What?" I could hear the confusion in his voice. "Her mother? How?"

"Biological, not adoptive. She thought he was her rapist."

"Who's rapist? Shelley's? Oh god, I'm so sorry John…."

"No … not Shelley, the Mum…. Look, this is too confusing over the phone. Can you come? Can you help?"

"I'm not sure if it's a conflict-of-interest, Mate but I'm sure they will tell me if it is. I'm on my way. Give me 40 minutes. I'll call ahead and tell them I'm her legal rep."

"Brilliant! Thanks, Mate." *I still cannot believe how Larry has gone from foe to friend.*

"Hang-on John, what's her name?"

"Gilling. Josephine Gilling."

"Ok great."

With that, the call ends and once again, I'm sat in my damp car, wiping away the water droplets and keeping watch.

Josephine

I am walked into the main body of the Police Station. Airlock after airlock. Each one opened with a swipe of the Detective's ID card. Then finally we enter the Custody Suite, and I'm ushered up to a high-level desk in the middle, of what looks like a reception area. It's noisy. There are numerous buzzers going off. I can hear what appears to be doors being banged, by presumably unhappy guests. There is a young lad sat on a side bench, he is wearing handcuffs, and he has a bloody nose; there is an officer sat next to him, scribbling something down into a small looking book. I look up at the desk and there is a grey wiry-haired, middle-aged officer sat at the other side.

"Well… then…" he says quizzically "What do we have here?"
"Sarge, Josephine here, has just handed herself in for the murder of Colin Joseph. Apparently, this took place

on 25th April 2018 in Bramley Wood.... arrested at 00:10 hours and ... relevant time? Well... That's about the same."

I'm asked to provide my full name, date of birth, and address.

"Ah... Ok ... Josephine... So, you are known to us, I've got a PNC record here... you've been arrested before then?"

"Me? No never!" I reply shocked.

"Ah yes, I make you right, but you have been reported as a Missing Person. Well... we can cancel that, definitely not missing, and it's clear to me that you are safe and well... There is no DNA on file. We will have to get that sorted."

The Sergeant carries on with the administration of getting me booked in, then he directs his questions back at the Detective.

"RIght then, that's done... Any reply to caution, significant statements?"

"Yes, she said "OK" to the caution after the arrest but, prior to that she said that "on 25th April 2018, I met a man called Colin Joseph at Bramley Wood, and I stabbed him to death and then I burnt the body. You have convicted Michelle Jones for this, but she didn't do it. I did. I am truly sorry."

"Did she now? Well, that's interesting... Did you say that?"

I look up and I nod my head.

Looking at the Detective, the Sergeant says, "Did you get that signed in your original notes?"

Appearing embarrassed, she replies... "No Sarge. I wasn't exactly expecting it. I didn't bring anything down with me, except a radio."

The Sergeant says nothing, but then starts frantically typing something up on the computer, he then pauses and looks at me.

"Right... I've typed up what you said on to the system. Do you want to read it?" He says this, pointing to a screen.... "and if you are happy, sign there." I read it.

It's what I had said word for word. I picked up the electronic pen thingy.

"Right then, sign away..."

I am then searched again!!! I am also asked a lot of questions about my well-being, and if I want the duty solicitor, or do I have my own?

I'm just about to reply that I don't have one, when a tall, ginger-haired and blue-uniformed officer talks over the Sergeant's shoulder, having only just come off the phone.

"Larry Heart is on his way for that one."

"Ah is he now. So, you have your own then? .... No problem."

I'm surprised at this, so I respond "Oh I do?"

Then after what seems like an age, I'm taken away from the desk to be "processed." That is what the ginger lad calls it, and I have my photo, fingerprints, and DNA taken. It is exactly like you see on the telly. Once this is done, I am walked down to a long corridor, past rows of solid blue doors, with black spy-holes, and then I'm told to go through the end door which is open. The ginger lad tells me about a buzzer, and that if I need anything, I only have to press it once, and that is it. He leaves me, and shuts the heavy door behind him. I take in my surroundings, and then I go and sit on what appears to be a concrete bed and then…. I wait.

DS Rachel Cooper

Well, I was not expecting that! I'm not even sure that I am ready. You would think having been with us for so long, that the cold cases would be good to go, but unfortunately, that is not really the case, and I have got some work to do and pronto! I had gotten a call from Custody. Apparently, the DNA profile that was on the knife has got a positive hit on the system. In addition, the female who has matched it forensically, has also just turned herself in; confessing to the murder of Colin Joseph. I can't believe it, if only all cases were this easy. It appears that the phantom from March has reappeared, and this time she is sat in a cell downstairs.

This week has already been long enough, and I was hoping to get my head down in the office as I'm CID Night Cover. Obviously, following on from what I have just learnt, that is not going to happen now. I call my DI to let him know what we've got, and to make sure that he is happy for me to run with this.

He stifles a yawn as he picks up the call... "Rachel? It's early or late, I'm not sure which. What can I do for you?"

"Yes, sorry Sir," (I call him Sir; feeling that this formality is appropriate, given the time of the call.) "I just wanted to make you aware, that a suspect has handed themselves in for the Colin Joseph Murder."

"The what murder? Sorry Rachel, is this a cold case?"

"Well .... Yes and no. It's the Body in the Wood Case...you know...the knife that Ma'am Gordon thought she had wiped fully clean; it still had the suspect's DNA on."

This has clearly woken him up, as he's instantly more questioning of my intended approach...

"And... are you OK to run with this? Have you got the Section 18 authorised? Do you want me to come in? Have you told the on-call DI? I take it that you are also preparing to interview re the linked series?" I feel like I have been assaulted due to the number of questions, that he has rapidly fired at me.

"Um ...yes, I've got Team Officers attending her address for the Section 18 search.... um... I don't think I need you in unless you want to be Lead Interviewer?"

"No that's fine. I don't think you'll get much done tonight anyway, well, not in terms of interview. It's late. It might be better to get prepped tonight, and then start afresh in the morning."

"I've also told DI Smith, he has just told me to use one of his officers in the Main Office as shotgun in the interview, and any fast time enquiries, he also said to pass them over to him.... and I've got all of the files from the other Forces, as I was already in the process of linking them together. My only Issue, Is that Larry Heart is down as her legal rep. But isn't that a conflict of interest? He represented Michelle Jones."

"Ah ok, no problem, you sound like you have it covered. Don't worry about Larry, I can call him from here. We go way back. I'll explain our concerns, and see what he says. I was only playing golf with him last week. Bloody bandit that one, there is no way he's off a 20."

His last comments are completely lost on me, presumably golf speak. I thank him and after the call ends, I get on with my interview prep.

John

I am still sat in the car outside the Nick. It was the right call having Shelley's mum stay over to look after the girls. I'm not really sure what I'm still sat here for, as I'm not even involved as such. It's just I feel that I can't leave. I need to be sure that this will lead to Shelley's release.

My phone rings, it's Larry.

"John?"
"Yes…"
"Larry here… Look, I'm not coming. I've had a call from Kev Smart. He thinks my involvement is definitely a conflict. He's told me to stay clear. I trust him. He's honest… Look, I've got a mate, I met him doing my training. Different firm, so no link to mine. He's good. I'll put the call into him and then declare my conflict,

and let custody know. Kev has also told me something very interesting... off the record of course."

"Go on..." I say... I was disappointed that I wouldn't have Larry as my inside man. We had really built a bond over all of this, and I had a renewed trust in him. He really was one of the good ones.

Larry continues...

"Gordon has gone. They've done her for perverting the course of justice, and gross misconduct in a public office..."

"What? When? How?"

"Early this morning apparently, and get this, it's all linked to Shelley's case... Things are moving in the right direction Mate... I'll sort out my replacement and give you an update when I can."

"Ok, thank you." My ears are still buzzing at the news... Those charges are indictable. She'll lose her job. She will go to prison.

"And John…. Go home. I know that you are still sat in your car. There is nothing you can do tonight."

The call ends, and I take his advice and I make my way home. Tomorrow I think, is going to be a much brighter day.

Josephine

I had been sat on the thin blue plastic mattress, on the concrete bed, for what seemed like forever. It was noisy outside of the cell, even though it was the middle of the night. One of the staff in the blue uniform, (I don't think they were a police officer, support staff maybe) had bought me in a blanket, and had dimmed the lights. I had tried to close my eyes briefly, but every time that I had nearly dozed off, the hatch on the door was opened, and someone would be looking in on me. I was so tired too. It must have been well over 48 hours since I had last slept. Since I'd had a shower and brushed my teeth even, and I could feel the build-up of fur on my teeth, as I rubbed my tongue over them. I felt wretched; not because of what I'd done, or where I was, I knew that I had done the right thing by coming back. It was just the sense of the unknown, and the fact that I wanted this to be over with.

I'm not sure what time it was, but the hatch is opened, (I later find out, that this is called a wicket) and the same scruffy Detective looks in who had originally arrested me... She didn't really talk TO me; it was more AT me...

"Josephine Gilling, I am also further arresting you for the murders of Paul Briggs, Eric Frost, and Geraint Pike which took place between 1984 and 1993. You do not have to say anything, but it may harm your defence, if you do not mention when questioned, something which you later rely on in court, and anything you do say may be given in evidence... OK?"

And with that, she has gone. She didn't even give me chance to reply... but to be honest, I couldn't anyway. I was speechless.

DS Rachel Cooper

I had got Emma to go down to Custody, and to further arrest her for the other murders. I knew that she had had the hump over it. I could tell immediately by her body-language. She had been sat at her desk, surrounded by a load of case files, head down, and typing. It was a very typical scene in CID these days. Overworked and under-appreciated. I knew that she had a good work ethic, but she was showing all of the signs of being burnt-out. She cared too much, and management; (even me in this case) didn't care enough. Crime was rising, so there were more victims, and more cases to deal with, and therefore; more and more pressure from the top! She had probably hoped for a quiet night so that she could get on with her backlog, and now she had got stuck helping me. Nevertheless, I needed it done. So, as is my right as her Superior Officer, down to Custody I sent her.

I actually think now, that I'm pretty much prepared. I've agreed to interview on behalf of the other Forces in relation to the historical cases, as well as the Colin Joseph one. Which should actually be a breeze…. After all, she has already admitted to that. Her legal rep has changed too. Kev sorted that out… She now has an Isaac Brown; I have actually never heard of him. Mind you, it's no bother. I have decided anyway that I will give full disclosure. He is due in for 9 am, and I am as prepped as I can be.

I look at my watch, and it is just after 6 am. It is too late to go home for a sleep, so I pull out the sleeping bag from under my desk, and I make my way to the conference room. I may as well try and get a little rest before the morning.

Josephine

It was morning and surprisingly I must have dozed off. I was awoken by the door opening, and a tall uniformed, middle-aged man, was stood in the doorway. He introduced himself as the PACE Inspector, whatever that meant. He said he was here to review me. I felt a little elated to see someone, other than the numerous pairs of eyes that had been watching me through the wicket. I just wanted to tell them what happened, and to get this over with. I was just about to start when he says...

"Right... I'm independent of the investigation and my role here is really to check on your welfare, so don't go saying anything about your case. You're detained so that we can interview you on tape, and that is happening later this morning." I say nothing, but I think he saw the disappointment in my face and so, he tries to lighten the conversation... "Right then, so how are you finding the room service? Have you put your order in for breakfast yet?"

"Um... no."

"Sorry, my little joke... So, have you been given food and water?"

I nod my head. They had given me a microwaved chicken korma when I had arrived, and a cup of tea, but both were still in the corner of my cell as I had had no appetite.

"......They will soon be around taking orders for breakfast... another microwave offering unfortunately..." He gives me a smile.

"I can see that your legal rep is booked for 9 am, so things should be happening soon... Is there anything you need to ask me?"

I say nothing... He continues.

"OK, then, so for now, I'm happy to authorise your further detention."

And with that, he steps back, closes the cell door, and is gone. 9 am can't come soon enough.

DS Rachel Cooper

I had gotten some sleep which was a bonus. I'm just freshening up in the toilets, as luckily, I always keep a fresh shirt, perfume, and toothbrush here. I have managed to look and more importantly smell quite nice. My mobile goes. It's Custody. Isaac Brown is at the Front Desk.

…. Right, let's get this show on the road.

DS Rachel Cooper

Isaac Brown was absolutely nothing of what I had imagined him to be. He was a smartly dressed, and a really softly spoken black guy in his 30's. He took a note of everything that I had told him on the Colin Joseph case; the facts that she'd handed herself in, that both his and her DNA was on a knife that had been handed in, in connection with the case. I also, unfortunately, had no choice, but to explain that the knife had been tampered with by another officer. He took it all in. I was surprised that his pen wasn't smoking by the end of it. It didn't stop on his page!

It was quite unusual, but it was like I had given him free access to the case-file ... a clear window. It was a disclosure unlike I had ever done before. Even with the simplistic of jobs, you usually held back a little. It is a game of cat and mouse. You conceal your winning hand, but this was very different. She had already confessed, and I felt this strategy was the right play.

The cold cases, however, they were a very different matter. The knife we had, had the potential to have delivered the fatal blows. Although, because of the destruction caused by the fires and degradation of their bodies, it was all inconclusive. Yes, the MO's were the same, but one case already had a conviction, (the victim's wife) so it could all just be a coincidence. All of that aside; it still felt right to me that she was responsible; there is no smoke without fire, as the old saying goes…. I also thought, well, she has coughed to one, why would she not cough to all of them? Anyway, after I had finished, I left him with his client, and I waited for my call to go back down for interview.

Josephine

The door springs open.

"Right, come on then, let's get you signed out."
"Sorry what? …. signed out of where? I've not said anything yet!" I'm feeling really unsettled, no one seems to want to hear what I've got to say. All this waiting around isn't helping Shelley.
"Yes, I know. I'm signing you out for your legal rep. Mr Brown is here. He has already done disclosure."
They might have well have been speaking another language to me, as I really didn't have a clue….

***

I'm led over to a side room. The Gaoler; which I now realise is the role of the blue attired officers, shouts over to the Custody Desk. "Sarge … She's with Mr Brown in Room 4. Is it marked up?"

"Yes, cheers Billy. All done."

I walk through the door, and I am greeted by a smart-looking black man. He smiles and reaches out a hand for me to shake.

"Ms Gilling, I'm very pleased to meet you. My name is Isaac Brown, and I have been asked by Larry Heart to represent you. I hope you are OK with that?" I shake his hand and whilst doing so I nod my head, to show my agreement.

"Well, we have a lot to get through. Take a seat please, Ms Gilling."

DS Rachel Cooper

Over an hour and a half has passed, and still no call. I had expected his consultation to be a quick in and out job. What was the delay? Had she changed her approach? Was she coerced into confessing? By the time that I had caught up with DI Smart, I had started to question my strategy. I had clearly disclosed too much. He had tried to reassure me, stating that he would have done the same, and to be patient, but I was tired, and as much as I shouldn't say it; I wanted this day over. I felt like I had a mountain to climb. This week had been eventful enough with dealing with Ma'am Gordon (I still can't call her anything else). So, I could have done without this today. Nevertheless, I still wanted it to be my best job yet.

My mobile rings. It's Custody.

"Shall we?" I say to DI Smart.
"Yep! Let's do this kid. You'll be fine!"

Josephine

I was exhausted even before we had started. Isaac was one of the most patient men that I think that I had ever met, well other than my father. In the brief time therefore, that I had known this man, I held him in very high regard. I told him everything and I cried, oh how I had cried. It was like the church confessional, and a therapy session all in one. He had advised me to split the arrests into two, so we concentrated on Colin Joseph initially, and I started at the very beginning. We put together a prepared statement. Isaac advised me that it was the best option. He said that I was clearly distressed, and it meant that I would not get flustered or confused. I would be in control, and I would get to tell my narrative. After all, I had already confessed. I was already going to be charged. Now, it was all about getting me the best possible outcome at court, and to do that, I needed to be consistent.

We also discussed the other murders that they had also arrested me for. I didn't tell him of my actual involvement in these deceased departures, for I felt no remorse. And from what Isaac knew about the evidence, the police had none. It was all circumstantial, and just a hunch of the Investigating Officer.

Apparently, there is a database that the police use called HOLMES. Hearing its name had instantly made me think of Conan Doyle's 'Sherlock - The Consulting Detective'. How I had loved reading his stories when I was growing up. Anyway, this HOLMES Database helps the police keep a track of all major incidents, like serial murders. It is across Forces, and if there is a pattern in circumstances, it will flag up. Isaac explained that since the Ian Huntley case (another monster), the Forces have been backfilling it with data, giving them a more cohesive approach.

Apparently, although historic, there was with the three other murders; a pattern. A formula that the killer used. This is known as their MO. The MO, Modus Operandi of Joseph's murder, had been practically a carbon copy of the other three historical cases, and HOLMES had identified this, and therefore it had put me firmly in the frame as being responsible for those too.

DS Rachel Cooper

I sign her out for Interview, and Kev and I make our way into Interview Room Number Four. I have got all of my exhibits, my questions, and my strategy. However, I am still half expecting that DI Smart will take over.

I am surprised when I look over at Gilling, at just how similar she is to Shelley Jones. She is practically her double. Her small frame, same coloured hair (obviously dyed), and the same piercing blue eyes. I feel like I have been here before. It's a real deja vu moment. Understandably, she looks tired, but it's more than that, she actually looks broken. I can see that she has been crying. She has blood-shot eyes and a blotchy face. She looks more like a victim, than any killer I've ever known. I get started.

"Right, ok then. Shall we begin? I know you've had some time with your Legal Advisor. Are you ready to

go? Do you need a drink? Comfort break?" Gilling shakes her head, and in a mouse-like voice she says...
"No, I'm fine. I just want to get this over with."
"Ok, then I am DS Rachel Cooper, and this is DI Kevin Smart. In a moment I'm going to switch on the machine. I will be recording this interview, both visually and audibly. I'll ask you to state your full name and your date of birth. I'll then remind you of what you've been arrested for, and the caution. Are you good to go?"
"Yes..." I switch it on, and the long beep of the tape recorder seems to take at least a decade to finish. I complete the legalities; day, date, time, and place. We each do our introductions for the tape, and then I remind her of why she's here and of the caution. She says that she understands, and then just as I'm about to start my first question, Isaac Brown cuts-in. He has a soft and silky voice that is instantly engaging.
"Sorry, DS Cooper to interrupt you, but my client as you know has already admitted to the murder and

prevention of lawful burial in relation to Mr Joseph, and she is extremely remorseful. We have prepared a written statement that should answer all of your questions, and may even provide enhanced clarity as to the circumstances. Would you permit me to read this aloud on behalf of my client? You cannot fail to see that she is in somewhat distress."

"Yes... OK, go ahead." I could have called this, of course, it's a prepared statement!

Josephine bows her head. She fixes her gaze on the floor as Isaac Brown clears his throat, and begins reading from the handwritten notes that he holds in his hands.

"I Josephine Gilling make this statement in relation to my arrest for the murder of Colin Joseph. I am aware that this may be used in evidence when this goes to

court. I wish to advise that on 25th April 2018, I met Colin Joseph at Bramley Wood. I stabbed him. I removed his fingertips, teeth and toes, wrapped him in a tarpaulin, and set his body on fire. I then left him in a shallow grave.

On 21st March 2019, I attended the Central Police Station and I provided a written confession to the murder, the murder weapon, namely a knife and a polaroid photograph of a male I knew in the late 1970's. This male, whom I knew as CJ at the time, and who I believed at the time of the murder to be Charlie

Jacobs, and not the now-deceased Colin Joseph.

In 1978 my father died suddenly. As my mother was heavily involved in the Church, she encouraged me too to become a member. The Church was located on the outskirts of Bramley Wood. CJ, a twenty-four-year-old man was an integral member of the local Youth Group and he took a shine to me. In the May of 1979 and aged 14 years old and whilst I was on a Church Youth Group Camping Trip, CJ brutally raped me at the rear of the Church at Bramley Wood. He held me down whilst reciting scriptures and forcefully took my virginity. I tried to tell my mother but she did not believe me. I then discovered that I was pregnant following the rape. I told my mother but due to the shame, she covered it up.

I ran away to give birth as a scared 15-year-old. I lied to hospital staff over my age, and as soon as I physically could, I took myself and my baby on a train up to Scotland and I abandoned my baby at "The Inn Public House". I left her there, along with my diary and an exact copy of the polaroid I'd handed to Police in the March of last year. The photo was of CJ and a boy called Barnaby.

On the same night after leaving my baby I took the train back towards the South. I then attempted suicide by stepping out in front of oncoming traffic. I was unsuccessful. This was not a cry for help. I wanted closure and to be safe again with my father. I was discovered and nursed back to health and returned to my mother.

Since then, I have never spoken of the rape, nor of the resulting child until I met up with Joseph.

The child I'd abandoned, I found out much later was called Michelle Jones, and after my mother had passed, I felt compelled to meet her. I went to her address to introduce myself. However, this never happened. I have never met my biological daughter.

Whilst at Michelle Jones' address, I was mistakenly handed my biological daughter's mail, and I discovered that a male with the same initials "CJ" and biological profile as my daughter, wanted to meet her.

I had thought that my rapist had wanted to meet my daughter and as I had never had closure, I reached out and arranged a meeting with CJ. However, what I didn't know was that Colin Joseph was the identical twin of Charlie Jacobs. The man who had actually molested me; and so, when I met Joseph and saw my attacker once again, I was back to being a scared 14-year-old girl and I stabbed him. I then disposed of his body.

I am truly remorseful of my actions. I now know what I did was wrong but at the time I had no control.

In relation to the murders of Paul Briggs, Eric Frost, and Geraint Pike, I do not take responsibility for their deaths... You'll find it signed and dated by my client."

Isaac finally finishes and looks expectantly over at me. I take a deep breath, having listened intently to everything that was read out, and I wipe a single tear from my eye. Her account was factual. There did not appear to be any elaboration or sugar-coating. She really was as every bit of a victim, as Joseph had been. It was a prepared statement like no other.

"Ok, well... thank you." I look over at the DI and even he looks shell-shocked. Neither of us had expected this. I don't feel like I have the strength, or willpower to carry on. What I have just heard has emotionally crippled me. That poor woman! Josephine is still fixated, staring at the floor, tears were streaming from her eyes. DI Smart speaks. "I think we need a break, don't you? Is ten minutes OK?... Interview paused at 11:15 hours."

Josephine

Both Officers leave the room, and I'm sat there with Isaac. My head is pounding. He grabs my hand. I would never normally let anyone so close, but I take his comfort. "You are doing well, take this break, and let's get you a drink, it will soon be over." He pops his head outside of the door to request a drink, but it must have already been organised, as two plastic cups of ice-cold water, are almost immediately delivered to us by one of the gaolers. I gulp mine down, but it fails to quench me, so Isaac gives me his. He has such a calm and soothing manner. I am so pleased that he has been sent to help me.

DS Rachel Cooper

As expected, when the interview was resumed, every question that I put to her was met with 'no comment'. I totally understood why. She had been through enough. I understood what drove her to it. Years of torment, no answers, but I also had a niggling feeling, that she was also somehow involved in those other historical cases. The only variation was Beachy Head. I had asked her about it, and it was the only question that she had forgotten to "no comment" on. She still replied in the negative, however, stating that she had never been. Not much more I can do now. I have just got to send my MG3 over to the CPS, and await their advice.

John

It had been a long night, and I have heard nothing. Shelley's mum has just gone home. She had stayed the night and she looked absolutely exhausted. I forget sometimes, just how much all of this must affect her too. Caring for our babies, whilst still worrying about her own

I am trying to force down a stale croissant that I found in the bread bin, when the girls run through the kitchen bickering over who's fidget spinner is whose. I didn't realise quite how on edge I was, as I erupt at the pair of them. They immediately stop arguing, and put the half-broken, bit of tut down on the counter. Their big blue-eyes clouded instantly by tears. I feel so guilty. I beckon them over. "Daddy is sorry. I didn't mean to shout." They have been through enough... "Shall we go and find the other one, and then you've both got one to play with?" They say nothing, just nod at me. I take their little hands, and I walk over with them to their playroom. God, it's a mess!! Temporarily my mind flicks back to Shelley. She would have had labels on all the drawers, and all the toys would have been away... When will this be over? I just need to know what is happening. I need her home. I need my family back together.

DS Rachel Cooper

The CPS came back to me pretty quickly. They asked if I wanted to split the case. On the Colin Joseph murder, there was sufficient evidence to charge. We had the murder weapon with the DNA, the confession, and the prepared statement. There was no denial, and she had taken full responsibility. This also meant that the conviction for Michelle Jones was to be immediately overturned. The CPS wouldn't authorise a charge for the unlawful burial, as they said it was all part and parcel of the murder. It made sense I suppose. On the historical cases, there was more work to be done. So, they have set me an action plan to complete ahead of any further consideration. So, over a well-needed coffee, I discussed everything with DI Smart and he agreed that we should run with what we had, and bail her on the rest.

John

I put my mobile down onto the kitchen side. I can't take it in. My head is buzzing. I cannot believe what I have just been told.

Rachel had called me….

She hadn't even charged her yet, but she had wanted me to be the first to know. The CPS are charging Shelley's biological mother, and they are fast-tracking the paperwork to have Shelley's conviction overturned. I don't realise it, but I am crying. I'm crying tears of fucking joy …. I've got to tell Shelley. Oh my god… I have got to tell her! It is almost over!

Josephine

I have finally been able to eat something, and microwaved chicken korma never tasted so good. I have been sat in my cell for the past two hours, and I had gotten used to the hourly interruptions of them looking through the wicket. To be honest, I looked forward to it. I was just thinking that my estimation skills must have been off, as the wicket is opened again, and surely not another hour has passed? I couldn't check as I didn't have my watch, they had taken that from me when I had arrived. I see that it is the female officer who interviewed me.

"Just checking that you are not on the loo." She says quite cheerfully.

"Ah OK, nope I'm not on the loo." She shuts her little spy-hole, and I hear the key in the lock. With the door now open she starts to speak.

"Ok, so I have been to the Crown Prosecution Service and they have authorised a charge."

"Oh OK, so what does that mean? Does Michelle get released?"

"Well…. Yes, it does." Her reply sounds a little surprised. I'm not sure why, as why else would I be here?

"Ok then. What do I do now?"

"Come with me to the desk. We need to formally charge you."

We walk back down the long corridor, and out to the hustle and bustle of the main custody area. I see Isaac, he is already stood over near a rather chubby looking Sergeant, who is sat behind the elevated desk.

"Are you OK? Do you know what is going on?" He asks me this softly.

"Yes… I'm being charged!" I say this almost jubilant.

"Yes, you are being charged in relation to the Colin Joseph case..." DS Cooper interrupts my and Isaac's conversation…. "and bailed on the others."

"The others?" … *I've got nothing to say about the others, why am I being bailed? I've admitted it... I feel flustered. I thought that they didn't have anything. I did this to save Michelle. Colin Joseph never deserved what happened to him, but the others. They were monsters.* My head is beginning to fog up, and Isaac must have seen my distress, as he places his hand gently on my shoulder.

"Josephine. It's procedure. Nothing to worry about. Let's get this sorted, and you out of here and we can talk afterwards, OK?"

"Ok... Sorry." My voice wobbles. I am nervous.

The Sergeant formally charges me for the murder of Colin Joseph. Once again, I'm cautioned and then advised of my first appearance date at court. What? They are letting me go? It's explained to me that so long as I surrender my passport, I would be bailed and actually free to go home. I just had to attend the court next week with my plea. It all seemed rather alien to me, why was I not going straight to prison? They then went on to explain that I was being bailed in relation to the other murders, and I was given a bail-to-return date for a fortnight's time.

None of it made sense to me. They were effectively letting me go. I signed everything that I needed to, and I was given back all of my property, except my passport. We walked out through the various airlocks, and back to the outside world. Isaac accompanied me throughout, until we were stood outside of the front of the Police Station. "Shall we go for a coffee?" He says and I nod.

DS Rachel Cooper

I'm done! Done for the day at least, and I am bloody shattered. What a 48-hours that I have had. I have spoken to her legal rep, and told him that I will formally record the rape and that if she wants to proceed, I'll organise a SOIT (Sexual Offences Investigative Trained) Officer to get in touch. He said he would discuss it with her, and get back to me. I have also got quite a bit to do to tie her to the cold cases, but I've got time. I decide that for now, however, I'm booking off.

I walk into the Green Bottle as I'm looking for a bit of me-time, in the company of a large white wine, and then suddenly, an eruption of claps greets me. It seems that most of D Team are in there… "Well done girl!" "I can't believe you got her!" I look around. "What? How did you know? The jungle drums have clearly been busy today. I've only just charged her…"

Then Paul, one of the old sweats pipes up "It's been a long time coming. I still don't know how she got as far as she did. Controlling bitch." A little confused, I reply... "What do you mean?"

"Always massaging the figures, taking advantage... and Management turning a blind eye. Well, other than Kev Smart that is. She has been on his radar for years... Well, she has fucked up this time.... Going to do time too. I don't envy her one little bit... Not with all the enemies that she'll have made over the years. They'll skin her!"

I finally twig, and I realise that they are talking about Ma'am Gordon. Someone must have really spilled the beans! They knew all about the knife, the "Police only" issued wipes, and her partial fingerprint…. They had so many conspiracy theories too. Mainly from the half-cut female officers… "Well, I reckon she got rid of her on purpose, to get back with John, you know they were once an item... probably off'ed that fella too, just to put her away. I wouldn't put it past her... She likes to take what isn't hers." The drunken officer is then hushed by her colleague, as she goes off on a rant about how Ma'am had taken advantage of her ex.

I had absolutely no idea just how hated she was, or how many times she had put pressure on officers to "make it fit." All the while keeping her own hands clean. No wonder my DI was so keen on nailing her. He had first noticed her antics years ago, but he had been unable to put together a case. She was the Force's very own Sweeney. I obviously put them right regarding my latest charge, making it clear that she wasn't a killer too. I felt it was only right to put to bed any further conspiracy theories! I also explained that the paperwork for having Shelley's charge overturned was being fast-tracked as we spoke.

"Ah well done Rach, John will be pleased. I've felt so awkward around him since…. Me and Megan were there at his Mrs' arrest… Ma'am was strutting about, all self-important…"

I nod my head and I take the praise, though I'm careful not to pass comment. I know all too well how dangerous that can be. The conversation then drifts off to who is shagging who, so I make my excuses and I leave.

Today had been a good day, and although I knew that I had not quite got the result that I had wanted, I still had the two weeks to rectify it. What I had learnt in all of this, is that I was only going to use what evidence I had available. No longer would we use the Ma'am Gordon's book of policing. I then thought of the embarrassment that one of the Senior Brass must be feeling, having sent her out to present her best practice. Someone somewhere would be considering an early retirement, I'm sure.

Josephine

I hadn't yet had the time, to process what had just happened. I had been officially charged with murder, but I was free to walk the streets, and even go to get a coffee.

It was strange, because I was also getting that coffee with a man. A man, that I had only met at most seven hours earlier. He had, in such a short time become so very important to me. We crossed the street and went into a little Italian Coffee Shop. Its name was "Nessun Fretta." I decided that this had been fate, and although I had wrongly translated it as "No Worries", and it had actually meant "No Rush", the sentiment was still the same, and I immediately felt relaxed in the warm, and sweet-smelling shop.

We took a booth, and Isaac went to get us a drink and a slice of cake. When he came back to the table, he laid out his purchases. I thanked him, and I tucked into the biggest bit of chocolate cake that I think I'd ever had. After my sugar levels had been nicely topped up, and with the caffeine beginning to kick in, we discussed my case.

He advised me not to worry about the historical cases. Telling me that by handing myself in, I had put them on the back foot, and they just wanted to be sure that they hadn't missed anything. I trusted him and I so wanted to tell him that it was me, and that the police were right. I had done it, but I also felt that maybe, I should keep that particular secret hidden. I just hoped that I hadn't left a crumb, a small forensic link that could prove that I was responsible. I knew, and I had already accepted, that I would go to prison for what I had done to Joseph. I deserved my punishment. He was Innocent in all of this. Unlike his vile brother.

Isaac reminded me of a Pastor. He had a naturally calming approach, and he seemed to see the good in me. He finished his coffee and put his hand on mine. "Josephine, we need to talk about the rape... DS Cooper has recorded it as a crime. Do you want to pursue it?" It was a bit of a shock "You mean criminally? Have him arrested? After all this time?"

"Yes, yes..." He soothes as he pats my hand.

"It's nothing to worry about, but it might give you some closure?"

I had not thought about doing anything through official channels in so long. My own mother didn't believe me, so why would the Police or a Jury? I think that is why I did what I did. It was just tragic that I had punished the wrong man. *Isaac continues, and says...*

"There's no rush, you can decide another day. I just wanted you to be aware of your options."

I thanked him, but I was feeling a little overwhelmed... I had been charged with murder, was on bail for another three, and now he wanted me to relive the rape all over again. I said I would think about it…

"Good that's all I ask. I think it would really help our defence."

We finish up, and he says he'll get his secretary to call with a date and time for me to meet my defence team. None of this sounds cheap, but luckily for me, I had not spent all of my money in trying to track HIM down, and I still had quite a lot of my savings which were left over from the sale of the house. My plan had obviously altered, but I knew getting my Michelle home, had to be my top priority.

John

Shelley was ecstatic when I told her. The relief in her face was instantly apparent, and she was clearly overjoyed at her impending release. The Governor had also advised that she had been made aware of the appeal, and so the transfer request had been cancelled. She would stay at the Unit whilst the slow wheels of bureaucracy turned, in order that every i was dotted, and every t crossed.

Her mood was also lifted due to the fact that I had met her biological mother. She had an uncontainable, and apparent delight at the fact that she too would be meeting her soon. She had instantly forgotten where she was, and who was ultimately responsible for that. Blood ties for Shelley were all that really mattered. In fact, Josephine had already been in touch. It was two days after she had been charged. The doorbell rang and

I went to answer it. She was stood there in the porch, and looking very sheepish.

"I wasn't sure if I should come."

I asked her why she had, and it was to do with her diary. She wondered if Shelley still had it, and if she did, would she mind if she took it? Obviously, it was hers and I knew exactly why she wanted it. It was clearly going to be key to her defence. I invited her into the kitchen whilst I went to find it.

"Here it is!" I said bringing it to her…. She held out her hands, and received it as if it were her most prized possession. She then pulled it into her chest, rubbing her hands over the outer cover, and then brought it up to her face to smell it.

"Well, I never thought I'd see this again… especially not at the time when I left it…"

She looks briefly ashamed, and then notices a number of loose pages.

"Oh, these aren't mine."

She's talking about the translations.

"Shelley worked out your cipher. They're the text decoded."

"Oh!" Sadness is apparent in her face.

"So, she knew then?"

"Yes, she worked it out when she was a teenager, I think."

"I feel awful. I always regretted leaving it with her. I don't really know what I was thinking." She is really apologetic, and I try to soothe her. I understand her a lot more now, since the first time that we had met. I have a lot of empathy, and as she looks so much like Shelley, I think I'm conditioned into caring for her.

"They want me to report the rape. You know.... They think it will help my case."

"You should. It will give you closure."

She smiles. "You're the second person to say that to me. Do you think Michelle would mind?"

"Why would she mind?"

"Well, she'll get stuck in the middle. It would all come out. Everyone would know."

I laugh... "It's a bit late for that, don't you think? She's currently locked up for murder, and everybody knows about that.... I think her involvement in the rape is relatively minor, don't you?!"

Her face colours up. "Sorry I'd not thought of it that way."

"No, I'm sorry ... 20 years in the Force has made me a little unfiltered... I can ask her, if that makes you feel happier?"

She smiles. I know she's Shelley's mother but she has a childlike quality. All the past influences have clearly left their mark.

"Ok, thanks for this. I'll be going now. Do you want my number so you can let me know?"

She scribbles down her landline. "I don't have a mobile. I lost it whilst I was away. When I get one, I can give that to you too."

"I've got an old phone that you can have if you like, in the meantime? It's a pay as you go? I had given it to the girls to play with, but I'm sure that they wouldn't mind...."

She smiles the exact same way as Shelley does, it explodes across her face. It was like I had offered her a million quid, and not a shitty old iPhone that was collecting dust in the playroom. "Well, if you're sure. That would be lovely... Thank you."

I nip off to get it, and she's left stood in the kitchen. I come back and she is admiring the artwork on the fridge door. "And these are the girl's pictures? They are wonderful. Can I ask, what are their names?"

"Maggie and Heidi."

"Oh, they are lovely names. I can't believe I have Grandchildren..."

"Yes, well, I suppose you do..."

I pass her the phone and charger, and she pops them into her bag along with the diary. She thanks me and starts walking towards the front door...

"Um… there is one thing. They said that I was a missing person when I was arrested. Do you know how that could be?"

"Well, someone reported you. I think from memory it was your boss at the Library. You just stopped turning up?"

"Ah, ok. That makes sense, I just couldn't work it out as it's just me, and I don't have any family."

I looked at her… "Well, that's all changed now."

I'm not sure if she was fishing for me to say it, but it didn't matter. I said it anyway. She was part of the family. I felt a connection, and I knew having her in Shelley's life would make a huge difference. It was just such a shame that soon they would be exchanging places.

Josephine

I was stood at the kitchen window this morning, washing up my breakfast things, and looking down into the garden below. I was engrossed in my thoughts about what I should do about the rape case. It made sense to go ahead with it, but what really could they do? I was so confused. Then all of a sudden something caught my eye. Flying up from the very far end of the garden, a robin. He flew right up to my window and perched on the window ledge. He actually made me jump. He stayed there for no longer than a minute, looked at me, and flew off again. I carried on with the washing up, and I was just drying my hands on a tea towel, when the mobile phone that John gave to me started to ring. It was him. I swiped the phone to answer.

"Hello"
"Hi, Josephine. It's John. Are you ok?"

"Um ... Hi John, is everything ok? Michelle? The girls?"

"Oh yes, nothing to worry about. I just thought I'd let you know that Shelley wants you to go ahead with the case, if you want to. She'll support you 100%"

"Really? Is she sure?"

"Yes, definitely, and she also wanted me to tell you that she can't wait to meet you."

"Oh, my goodness really? Even after all I've done?"

"Yes, Josephine. You're her mother." I felt so warm, so loved. I never thought I'd be considered her mother. Not after everything.

"Ok, wonderful. Thank you. I'm meeting my defence team later with Isaac. I'll tell him."

"Great."

"John. Thank you so much for your call." The call ends and I'm back to looking out of the window, and my robin is back. I just know that he's my dad. He had come to tell me that everything is going to be ok.

DS Rachel Cooper

I sent off the knife again. The CPS want further comparisons to the photographed remains, to see if any of the striations are a match. I was told the first time, that due to the high temperature of the fire, that the bone fragments were in a very poor condition. They had already said it was difficult to say categorically that it was the same knife used, but never the less I did what was requested, and I put it forward for further analysis. The first report was conclusive over the DNA that it held. Just Joseph's and Gilling's. She must have nicked herself at the time of his murder. It still amazes me that she kept the knife. Why go to all of the trouble of disposing of the body, and any identifying features, but retain the one thing that proves that you did it?

I was equally surprised that they had managed to identify the bodies of Briggs and Pike. They had been UNIDENT for years. The forensic advances over the past couple of years had been immense. I just wished that they could get me that final piece of the puzzle. I knew it in my gut, that she was linked to these cases. There were too many common themes.

All charged with paedophilia, but not one of them convicted.
All stabbed; identifying features removed, and bodies burned.
All found in remote woodland.
All wrapped in tarpaulin.

Beachy Head was the only inconsistency; my stumbling block. She had said that she had never been, and I would be hard pushed to prove otherwise. The search team at her flat had found nothing.

Also, she didn't seem to have any connections to the deceased. With Pike, he was from Exeter, and only moved up after being harassed by the local vigilantes...

There was nothing to suggest that their paths had crossed, even though he had relocated close by. Briggs was from, and had been found in a neighbouring county. I think he had relocated briefly to a local guesthouse, but again, there was nothing to suggest that they had ever met....and Frost? Well... his wife is currently at HMP Featherwater, having been convicted for his murder, and she has got a motive. He had sexually abused her daughter, and an eyewitness had put her at Beachy Head. Maybe I'm just too close to this, maybe I am just barking up the wrong tree.

Josephine

Today was the day, I had been given the address of where I needed to be by Isaac's Secretary. I caught the 08:30 train, and I was full of anticipation. I was to meet a barrister by the name of William Bell, and Isaac would be there too.

I walked out of Bank Station, following the route that my iPhone had given. As I emerged, I realised that I had been here before. Crossing the road left and right, I came to the very square that I had sat in, all those years ago to eat my ham and pickle sandwiches. I looked for the building number that I was to attend, No.298. Oh, my goodness! I couldn't believe that I hadn't realised that the Chambers who were to represent me, were those of John Allott Abrahams QC. I was then very briefly, catapulted back to our sitting room, all those years ago with Mother. Both of us sat watching the TV, and her saying "Well... you know they have done it, if he is representing them...." I smiled at the irony.

I walked up to the grand building, with a rather bizarre and relaxed feeling of familiarity. In through the doors, and over to the reception, and who should I bump into? Robbie! The Clerk. He had not retired as I might have expected.... He was still there. A lot older obviously, a lot less hair, but still every bit as scruffy. He was now the Chief Clerk, and I'm sure that had come with a hefty pay rise and yes, he was still in control. He was still responsible for getting in the business; and this time, I was his business. Without even thinking, and forgetting that I was not the teenage work experience girl, who had only spent four days there. Yes... four days and that was well over 30 years ago. I said "Robbie! Hi!"
He observed me, and appearing as harassed as ever, he seemed not to recognise me. Why would he?! "Oh, hello? Um... can I help you? Do you have an appointment?" Just as he finishes his questions, and as

he tries to work out where he can direct me, in walks Isaac, through the grand doors.

"Ah…. Wonderful!" he says. "You've met. Josephine is who I was talking about. The one you've allocated William to deal with."

"Ah, yes of course. Come with me. Pleased to meet you, Josephine. We know all about your case, and we think we can definitely help."

I smile at him, and as I'm not sure of the etiquette and whether I should actually tell him that we have met before, I say nothing. I simply follow him in through a door, and into a glass-walled office. The shell of the Chambers is still the same, but inside has definitely been modernised since my last visit.

I'm introduced to Mr Bell. He's a grey-haired Barrister. Slightly overweight, but because of his height he carries it well. He wastes absolutely no time in discussing the case. Time as they say, is money.

"Right then Josephine. I understand that you've got yourself in some trouble, and we'd like to try and help you to lessen the extent of your sentence. We, therefore, want to discuss the possibility of a not guilty plea. What do you think?"

"Not guilty? But I am guilty. I did it. I've already said so."

I look over at Isaac, as I am so confused at all of this.

"Listen to him, Josephine. It's a strategy. We want to help you. You are as much of a victim in all of this, as is Joseph." I nod my head and decide to hear them out.

After well over an hour, I fully understand what my defence is going to be. They have proposed that I'm not guilty by reason of diminished responsibility. Mr Bell explains that we would need to have me psychologically assessed, as he is pretty sure that I've been suffering from Post Traumatic Stress Disorder, a condition that he thinks I have had, ever since the rape and the birth of Michelle.

"Think about it, when you saw Joseph that day, all you saw was your attacker. You could not distinguish between him and Jacobs. You acted on the impulses of a frightened 14-year-old girl... Maybe if you'd been supported throughout your childhood, and into your adult life, and had the appropriate counselling and therapy, this would never have happened.   You are not at fault...."

He then cited a number of cases, and in particular **Swet v. Parsley Lord Diplock** and **R v Byrne (1960)**. It actually made sense to me. Yes, I had met him that day, but I don't think I had meant to kill him. I had the knife for protection. Part of me felt, or knew that I was maybe reinventing my narrative, but perhaps that was what I had to do. I had after all, already been punished enough.

We also discussed the rape, and what I was going to do. Isaac was so pleased when I said that I wanted to go ahead. "Wonderful. I'll let DS Cooper know and she'll liaise with the Sexual Offences Team."

"I've got this too..." I said as I pulled out the diary. It's written in code, but it details what happened to me that night... With the rape I mean." Mr Bell and Isaac agreed that it would be integral evidence for both cases; that and of course, Michelle. Her mere existence proved that I was underage, and legally I could never have consented. I could see now how reporting the rape officially, was intrinsic to my defence.

DS Rachel Cooper

It was highly unprofessional I know, but I'd gotten friendly with John, since the time that he had brought me that note. Anyway, I saw him in the corridor, on route to my face-to-face with the CPS Prosecutor. I smiled at him and before I realised what I was saying, I had blurted out...

"Hi John, how are you, and that murderous mother-in-law?!" I think he got the joke and he gave a laugh...
"Yes, all fine. She's actually quite nice for a cold-blooded killer."
"Talking of the devil," I say... "I'm actually en route to see the CPS."
I flash at him the named case files, as if to demonstrate my providence.
"Ah, good luck with that. I suppose, in for a penny and all that."

"Ha!" I laugh, "Ah thanks. I'm not holding my breath. Between you and me, I can't link her to any of the males, and she said that she's never even been to Beachy Head! Anyway, I'm definitely sure that I really shouldn't be discussing any of this with you... How's Shelley by the way?"

"Well, she's actually rather good considering that she's still locked up. We are so quick to put them away, not so much, however, when it comes to sorting out their release. The wheels of bureaucracy move at a snail's pace... Actually, I was meaning to ask you. Is there a date yet for Gordon's case?"

"Well... She's pleaded not guilty, and there's a backlog at the courts at the moment. Five, six months, I think it's scheduled for. I've got it written down in my paper diary. I can check later if you like." John laughs at me. "Paper diary? You need to get with the times' girl! ... No, it's fine. Anyway, I've got to get off. School run and all."

"Yes, me too."

"Ah yes. I suppose I should wish you luck... break a leg."

I smiled and walked away. "Break a leg" … Yes, to be honest, this is all very much like a Shakespearean tragedy. There are to be no winners here.

Josephine

I went into the Police Station and I gave my statement. It was very strange being back. This time, I asked for a DC Groves. She worked in the Sexual Offences Team. She met me in the Front Office, and again I was taken through a number of airlocks. This time, however, not through to Custody, but to an area that had been set out like a front room. There was a comfy looking yellow sofa, and an armchair positioned adjacent to it. A large leafy pot plant sat in the corner and a coffee table with tissues and bottles of water on it. I think that the only thing that really gave it away that it was an interview room, was the camera that was pointed directly at the sofa, and the numerous black dots which I was told were microphones.

DC Groves was young, and no more than 25 years-old. She had long brown hair and a sharply cut fringe. She was dressed in tailored blue trousers, which were teamed with a bright yellow knitted jumper with gold buttons on the shoulders. She had looked nothing like the officers that I'd come across to date, although she was still every bit as professional.

DC Groves explained the whole process to me, and as to why we were videoing my interview. She put me completely at ease, explaining that rather than take the stand at court, the judge can rule that the video statement is used. "It's to prevent any further distress," she said... And it made complete sense. It was a shame that this wasn't best practice in the 1980's. Briggs might have been saved, and behind bars rather than being buried six foot under. Punishment was punishment in my book, no matter how it was delivered.

DC Groves took me through everything very slowly, and we started at the very beginning. We focused initially on the death of my dad and how that had made me feel. I was immediately just like a little girl again. So lost. I had so much emotion and I was in so much pain.

We then moved on to the Church, and my involvement and how the youth group had given me structure and a focus. We discussed my friendships and my hopes of a relationship with Barnaby, and with hindsight, I saw the obvious grooming of me by CJ. At that time, I was so naive, so innocent.

DC Groves ensured that I took plenty of breaks. I drank so much water, it was needed. As soon as I'd taken a sip, it seemed to bubble up again and straight out of my eyes. I just couldn't stop crying. I was then asked to speak about that night. It was unbearable. I screamed, I even punched out. I felt like I was back there. Reliving every painful moment. My emotions were raw as I told her of the pregnancy and how frightened I had been. The pain and the shame of Michelle's abandonment, but also the feeling that I had absolutely no choice. It was the same feeling that I had when I walked out into the motorway. I was in utter despair. I wanted it all to end.

Once the interview was concluded and having wiped away my tears, and blown my nose, for which must have been the one-hundredth time. I just sat there. I felt like I'd been assaulted. I felt small, vulnerable, and completely exhausted. DC Groves told me how well I'd done, how brave I was, and that she was committed to getting me justice. I thanked her, and I asked if that was it? She said "Yes, for now…" but then I remembered about the diary.
"I've got this. It's my diary from when I was a girl. It's written in code, but it's easy to decipher." Her eyes practically lit up.
"Oh, my goodness, yes! Show me. It's like your original notes. It's certain to help." I wasn't really sure what she meant about original notes, but I gave it to her

anyway. She started to read over it, and then I stopped her...

"Um actually, do you mind if you just copy it for now, so you can see if it will help. It sounds silly, but it's rather sentimental."

"Of course. Look, I'll take a copy of the pages and you can exhibit them. OK?"

"Um... Yes ok." I still wasn't down with the lingo.

"What are these pages?" She pointed to the loose sheets.

"Oh, they are actually the pages that have been decoded. My daughter worked it out, and she translated it. They are probably of more use to you than the actual diary."

"Ok then, I'll take a copy of each... And do you have the contact details of your daughter? I need to speak to her. Get her DNA, her statement...." I smiled, thinking...
You are not telling me that you don't know who my daughter is, or how I came to be here .... She had obviously opted to treat me wholly as a victim, and to

not let anything that she had heard on the grapevine change how she dealt with my case. She didn't mention it and neither did I.

"Well, she's not available at the moment, but as soon as she is, she'll definitely get in touch."

It had been the most harrowing of afternoons, but I knew that I had done the right thing.

DS Rachel Cooper

It was as expected. I had argued my case but the lawyer couldn't be convinced.

"Rachel, it's all circumstantial. What's not to say that someone somewhere, hasn't written about the other murders, and she's just copied it. Consciously or subconsciously. She may not even be aware of it herself. You said she was a trauma victim. It just doesn't satisfy the Threshold Test." I nodded my head.
"Yes, I know, but I just feel that she's connected. They were all paedophiles. Admittedly without convictions. It's the exact same MO as Joseph's death. The man she thought had abused her... It's way too much of a coincidence!"
"I hear what you are saying, and you are probably right but without the evidence... Look, you know she's admitted to Joseph's. She's going to get a custodial. You might just have to satisfy yourself with that."

I left the meeting very UN-satisfied. Until I'd sat down to the face-to-face meeting, I really had no idea how strongly I felt, and how sure I was that she was responsible for these murders too. Without the evidence however, I knew there was nothing that I could do. Every avenue that I had tried, I had come up empty-handed. The search at her address yielded nothing of note. The knife couldn't be conclusively linked.... and I had absolutely no means of connecting her to any of the deceased. I had to let it go. I walked slowly back to the office. I may as well cancel her bail back date. Begrudgingly I put in the request for "No Further Action due to insufficient evidence, as per CPS guidance".

Josephine

It had been a busy few days. Isaac had called me to tell me that my bail date, for the other three murders had been cancelled. I'd been "eliminated" from their enquiries. I felt so relieved. I had also been to court for my first hearing, and I had entered my plea. It was over in a flash and I had been so nervous. I met Mr Bell and Isaac outside, and they had tried to reassure me that it was just a formality …. and it was. I'd had butterflies in my stomach. I couldn't stop going to the toilet, but I was in and out of that courtroom in a second. I stated my name and address, entered my not guilty plea and that was it, over and done with. I was advised that due to the seriousness of my case. It had been directed to the Crown Court and a date was set for six months' time. In addition, and luckily for me, the prosecution also lodged no concerns over me remaining out on bail, so essentially, I was still a free woman. After the hearing, I thanked Isaac and Mr Bell. He hadn't really needed to come, but he had advised that he felt emotionally attached to my case, so had wanted to support me.

Anyway, after I had left them, I was walking along the street, near to the library, and as I looked up, I saw my car. I had forgotten all about it, and I was shocked that it hadn't been towed away by the council. It was covered in leaves and there was a significant amount of bird muck on it, but it still looked roadworthy. Well, other than a flat tyre. I felt in my handbag and to my absolute amazement, it still contained the spare key. I pressed the button on the fob and immediately it sprung to life as I heard it unlock, along with the flash of the indicators. Even more amazing was that when I put the key in the ignition it started!

I was still dressed in my suit, so not exactly looking the part for changing a tyre, but nevertheless, I set to work. Then I heard a familiar voice.

"Oh, my goodness, Josephine, it's really you!"

I looked up, still holding the jack that I had just got out of the boot, and I saw it was Imogen; my boss from the library. She flung herself around me.

"I thought something terrible had happened… I reported you as missing to the police!"

"Oh, Imogen!"

"How are you?"

"I'm fine, I'm fine…. I didn't mean to worry you."

"They went to your flat, they said it looked like you had gone away. I'm so glad that you are safe." She steps back and looks at me again. Clearly noting the suit. "Oh, and you've had a loss? Whose funeral? Look, if I can be of any help?" I wasn't sure what to say. I just nodded and said thank you. I didn't think that I was really ready to tell her where I had really been, or why.

"Look, I know you are busy…" She says looking at the flat tyre. "Come in and see me. We still haven't replaced you, so you might even consider coming back?" I thanked her again, I didn't know what else to say. As she walked off, I started to cry. The stress of the day and her kindness had all been too much.

Five months later

Shelley

Finally, the day had come. After months and months of waiting, my appeal was heard and my conviction for murder was ruled to be unsafe. It had been a long time coming. I had assumed that once Jo and my mother had been charged, I would have had a ticket out of here. The wait had only been bearable because I knew it was coming.

The months that had passed whilst I was still at the unit, I used wisely. I utilised all of the facilities, taking full advantage of the extended physio, and the counselling sessions that they offered. Although I seemed to need the counselling less and less these days. I hadn't met my biological mother yet, but just knowing that she came back to save me, it had meant so much. All my life I had felt disposed of. I felt like a waste product. I hadn't once considered that she left me there, all alone, to save me. It made such a difference. I had also spoken to my mum about her. I didn't want her to think that I didn't need her anymore. She would always be my mum. It was just that Josephine, she made me feel complete somehow.

Tomorrow was the day and I had packed my bags. John was due to pick me up and finally take me home.

Tomorrow I would be a free woman.

Tomorrow night, I would bath my babies, read them their stories and tuck them into bed. It felt like a fairy story, not just because of what I had been through, but I was finally going to get my happily-ever-after. I was eventually going to meet my mum.

John

She was coming home.

There was an excited charge buzzing all around the house, and I had put up both banners and balloons. I had also bought a cake, put sweets out into bowls, and the prosecco was already chilling in the fridge.

This was a celebration.

I had decided that I would order a pizza once she was home, as I didn't think it was right that I tried to cook. No, I wouldn't be inflicting Shelley with one of my inevitably inedible creations. I expect the girls just wanted their mummy home, just so their dinner times were once more enjoyable!

Anyway, the welcoming committee only consisted of Shelley's mum and dad, and obviously Heidi and

Maggie. I had decided against a party. I knew Shelley. All she would care about was us being there. She was never one for big gatherings. She always said that our Wedding Day with a guest list of 90, had been 88 people too many!

I picked her up at ten o'clock sharp, and I carried her bags for her. Although her mobility was pretty much back to what it was before, to the trained eye you could spot a very slight paralysis in the way that she now walked. A hangover, and an unfortunate reminder of the injuries that she had inflicted on her neck. When we were out in the fresh air she stopped, taking the biggest of deep breaths.
"Are you ok?"
"I AM, actually and I can't believe what has happened. You just couldn't write it... John, I'm free!"
"Yes, you are, Baby" I say grabbing her hand and squeezing it tight. It feels simply amazing to have her with me. Not locked up, not being looked at, and our

every interaction monitored. Since she had been inside, I think that I had felt every much a prisoner as her.

I put her bags into the boot of the car. She is already sat in the passenger seat. Whilst getting in the driver's seat, and strapping in I say "Right, shall we go home? The girls are beside themselves. They were running about like mad things this morning."
To be honest, I wasn't sure if that was the excitement of having their mummy home, or the number of Smarties and Chocolate Buttons that they had consumed; sneaking them out from the bowls that I had put out!
Shelley looked at me "Um… Do you mind if we don't?"
"What?" Confusion clearly written all over my face.
"It's just… I want to see her first. I've waited all of my life, and I know that I haven't got long."
"Josephine, you mean? Your mum?"
"Yes! Does it sound silly or wrong that I want to see her first, when my babies are so excited?" I confessed to

her, that their excitement may have been chocolate induced...

"So, can we?" She asked again.

"I don't see why not? Look, let me call her and make sure that she is in."

I got out of the car. I had obviously realised that she would want to see her mum, but I didn't think that she would want to straight away…. In fact, I had actively put Josephine off, thinking it would be too much for her immediately after being released. I make the call and she answers it straight away.

"John! How is she? Have you got her? Is she out?"

"Yes, she's out. She's asked to see you. Can we come?"

"What, now?" There is a slight panic or hesitation in her voice, I can't tell which. Then she responds, "Yes, yes come. I can't wait to see her!"

Josephine

Oh, my goodness. They have just called me. They are on their way. I am going to finally see her again. It has been 40 years, and I'm going to actually talk to my baby. My stomach is in knots, and my heart is racing. I feel like I'm a kid again with my dad. It is like we have put a bet on and we're waiting for our horse to come in.

My adrenaline is pumping.

It seems to take forever for them to arrive, and then the buzzer goes. I press the door release and I can hear their footsteps as they walk up the stairs. I had opened the door before she had a chance to press the bell and there, on the landing, stood before me, is my daughter. My Michelle.

"Hello, Mum!"

I throw my arms around her, tears of joy escaping from my eyes. For the first time in years, it had felt natural to be so close to another person.

"I'm so sorry, I'm so, so sorry!" Her embrace is just as tight as my own.

"It doesn't matter, it's over now. I've finally met you." We stand as one for at least five minutes, neither one of us wanting to let the other one go. John is behind her, clearly feeling uncomfortable, just stood.

"Right then, are we coming in? Is a seat and a cuppa in the offing?" You can tell he's a policeman, not shy in asking for a cup of tea!

"Yes, of course, come in."

I brew up, I've only got a half-eaten pack of rich tea biscuits to offer them. I wasn't expecting any company. This is a very unusual event for me.

The only occasions that I ever do have company is when the boiler is read, or when Jehovah's Witnesses manage to by-pass the intercom, but I would certainly never invite either of them in for a cuppa and a biscuit!

We sit down in the lounge. It is silent. John speaks first, "Lovely cuppa, best that I've had I think." Shelley nods, but there is an awkwardness to her.
"Um, I really am sorry you know," I say this not knowing what else to say.
"I know Mum and really I don't mind. It's all water under the bridge. I think...." *She stumbles with what to say*... "Um … I think I have wanted this for so long. I just don't know what to say. I'm a bit shell-shocked, I think." I knew exactly what she meant, and I still feel so guilty for what I've put her through.
"Did John tell you? My case, it starts next month." She nods, her eyes beginning to well up. "And that's the problem. I have only just found you, and I am going to lose you again soon."
It was strange, my motherly instinct had kicked in. I wanted to soothe her. Immediately, I reply. "You'll not

lose me, you never did. I have always been here; I was just worried that I wouldn't be good enough. I was damaged. I didn't want you to be part of that...." I start to ramble... "I regret leaving you with that diary. I always will. You never needed to know. I'm so, so sorry."

We are both sobbing. Both emotional messes. John looks over. He's just slurped the last of his tea.
"Right, are you two going to stop anytime soon? I don't think I've got the skills to build an ark!" We both laugh at this.
"Look, Mum, I've got to go, but I want to get to know you. Get to know you properly. Can we meet? You can come to the house, or I'll come here? Go out for coffee and cake, we've got so much to catch up on. Whatever you fancy. I just know that I need you in my life..."
It was music to my ears, and I hugged her once more before she left. I hadn't felt this joyful, since before Dad had died, and I was a little girl.

One Month Later

Superintendent Jo Gordon

Look at them treating me as a pariah! All of them thinking that this is a spectator sport. It's not, it's my fucking life! Bastards, every one of them. I look up at the public gallery, and I think I recognise practically every one of them. Well almost all, except one or two. Presumably journalists. They can piss off too, making money out of other people's misery.

My case, god knows why is of public interest! Where was the public interest, in all those years of personal sacrifice? Long days and nights, keeping the public safe and putting the criminals behind bars?!

It's like the whole of the Force has turned out for this one day. They have forgotten that I made them. Most of them wouldn't be where they are without me!

For two weeks, I've turned up, and I have listened to how corrupt I am. How what a terrible job I did. What a terrible person I am. It's all bullshit. I did everything for that job, those victims. I got them justice. That was all me! Commendation after commendation. Conviction after conviction. I don't even see the issue. It was one small blip in a seemingly perfect career. She didn't bloody die, did she! She's out now anyway, so I really don't see what the problem is!

I know exactly who to blame. This is all of her fault. I wish I'd never met her, never helped her, never given her a chance.

I am so distracted, that I almost don't hear the Court Clerk issuing his instruction. I'm told to stand as the Foreman of the Jury delivers the verdict.

Standing tall and looking straight ahead, I hear the damning words of "Guilty Your Honour."

Shelley

This past month has been brilliant. Mum and Mum, both met. My goodness, they got on so well. I was worried that Mum, would somehow feel threatened by Josephine, but she wasn't. My mum is just so amazing. She actually spoke to me after Josephine had gone home for the night. I was in the kitchen and just washing up, which is still somewhat a novelty that has yet to wear off! We'd all had dinner together, and she has grabbed hold of my hands. I still had my rubber gloves on, so it felt a little weird but she says "Darling I'm so glad that you've met her. I've seen a change in you. An inner peace...." The conversation seemed a little deep for an eight o'clock, on a Wednesday night so I lightened it ... "Well Mum, that's probably because I'm not a convicted murderer anymore, my washing up's done, and there's a half bottle of wine in the other room with my name on it!"

"I'm serious Shelley. I'm glad that she's in your life, in all of our lives, and no matter what happens at the trial, she always will be. Ever since we were blessed with you in our lives, all I've ever wanted is for you to be happy." With that, she pulled me closer to her, and she kissed me on the forehead. That was my mum through and through; always supportive, and always with my best interests at heart. Even though Josephine had the potential of pushing her aside, Mum rejected her own fear in support of me. I knew however that was something that would never happen. My mum would always be my mum. No matter what.

Josephine had also met my babies, and they had instantly taken to her. It was a difficult decision as to whether they should get acquainted, as we all knew it would be a brief encounter. I'd already made the decision that no matter where she was sent to, I'd visit but, I'd leave them out of it. The girls had had enough prison visits to last them a lifetime.

The Dean of the University, he also contacted me when he had heard of my release. He rang personally to offer me a position. I just couldn't believe it. I didn't think I'd have any worth, having been out of it for so long. Research is a tough field. After a break, you will undoubtedly have missed out on a technique, or a breakthrough. You will always be playing catch-up. That aside however, he was very complimentary "You have natural talent. That coupled with your modesty, means that you, as you have previously, will continue to achieve great things. The University would be proud to support you in your work... Just think about it. Our door is always open...." I told John about the conversation. His face erupted with pride. He always said that I should never have left. "See, so they know your worth... I just wished you did!" I suppose that I have never felt good enough. I thought any break-through that I had, had been lucky rather than as a direct result of me, and my hard work. I had actually discovered in the unit, after hours of counselling, that I suffered from "Imposter Syndrome." It certainly made sense, as it was associated with both anxiety and depression. Both of which I had experienced throughout my life. Anyway, I will go back to the University, but not yet. For now, I'm enjoying spending time out in the fresh air, getting to know my mum, and spending time with the girls and John. Life really couldn't be any better!

John

It has all been so natural. I can't believe how well she has adapted to being home. The one thing with Shelley is that she hates change; any type of change. Now, I know going from being locked up, to being free, is usually always seen as a good thing, but for Shelley, I was worried it would derail her, especially with the addition of her mum.

This month has been really rather intense. Their relationship has certainly advanced quickly. Josephine has been over to the house practically every day. God, I'm so glad that we never moved. She lives literally around the corner. I can sometimes see the desperation in Shelley, as she tries to cram her 40 years of loss into just 30 days. It all seems so unfair. They think that the case will attract a lot of media attention. Therefore, it's been moved to the Old Bailey. It's all becoming rather a worry. I hope Shelley can cope with all this.

Jo Gordon was sentenced. I went to watch. Shelley couldn't. What that woman put us through! Well, it's not worth thinking about...and for what reason? Self-gain? Promotion? Jealousy? I still can't believe that she almost cost Shelley her life. Well, she has lost hers now. She was given life, with a tariff of 15 years. The Judge clearly wanted to make an example out of her. To send out a clear message. She is now the one in segregation at HMP Lightbridge. For her own protection of course. Mind you, it's only a matter of time before she cracks. Not that it matters to me, they can throw away the key for all I care!

Josephine

Over the past months my defence team haven't stopped. They sent me for a Psychiatric Assessment, and I have finally been diagnosed with PTSD. Isaac was so pleased when he heard. He rang me up personally. His soothing voice ... "It's what we all knew Josephine, but now it's official. It's a diagnosis. It's the backbone of your defence."

They have also sought witness after witness to testify on my behalf. They have been so thorough, even locating one of the barmaids at Dad's old local. Demonstrating that once, I had been a carefree sociable child. I read the list of names, all willing to help me and I felt humbled. A retired nurse, who had looked after me at the hospital after I'd tried to kill myself. A now, very elderly Parishioner from the Church; she had apparently had suspicions over CJ, but hadn't said anything. She said she would carry the guilt of not speaking up, until her dying day. It was strange. It felt as if this case were all built on showing what CJ had done to me, and nothing to do with the fact that I had stabbed an innocent man to death. I was assured by Isaac however, that they had the right defence strategy and to trust Mr Bell and his team.

DS Rachel Cooper

I have had quite a successful morning so far working on my latest case. I have finally put the "Josephine Gilling" Cold Cases to bed. I can't keep going over the same case files. I know that I've followed up every lead, every crumb and there just isn't enough for the CPS.

It's just gone 11:30 am, and I'm feeling rather peckish, so I nip to the canteen for a very naughty '999 Breakfast'. I needed to be quick before they stop serving it, ahead of the lunchtime menu. I'm just tucking into my calorific treat of eggs, bacon, beans, toast, and sausage when I spot DC Groves.
"Kate! How are you?"
"Hi Rachel! Yes, you know, busy, busy! I get one off my work-file and another 6 appear!"
"How's Cold Cases? Are you still enjoying it?"
"Yes and no, it can be rather frustrating. Lost evidence, etc. It's so hard to get anything past the CPS. They

seem to want a 100% assurance of a conviction before you get any sniff of a charge!"

"You want to try working in my unit…" She laughs…

"Bloody nightmare! Any hint that the victim was drunk, any slight suggestion of initial consent, and they just won't proceed. It is soul-destroying for me, let alone for my victims."

"Actually, talking about victims, did Josephine Gilling ever come and see you?"

"Yes, yes, she did, and to be honest that is the one case that I know the CPS wouldn't hesitate to charge... That file is ready to go. I've got the Forensic Reports confirming the DNA. Statements from her, and her daughter. He's circulated as wanted, and I've got the Warrants Team tracking him down. …. He might actually be my first extradition. They think he's overseas."

"Well, that is exciting! You'll have to let me know how you get on."

Florence our wonderful cook, calls out to Kate…

"Darling, your scrambled eggs is ready!"

"Right gotta go, I've got a victim in ten minutes. I need to shovel that down pronto…. No rest for the wicked hey..." She laughs as she says this, and then goes to get her breakfast from the counter.

John

I cannot believe how easily she has transitioned back to normality. I know that her time in prison had been relatively short, but it was no less traumatic. Since her release, she seems to be a new and improved version of herself. I know that this change in her, is by and large due to getting to know her real mother. Being abandoned like she was, it had haunted her for all of her life. She had always felt like she didn't belong. Patty and Colin, they did their best, and I know that they love her with all their hearts, but I think she has always felt like an outsider. I can see that she is finally happy, and from now on, I am going to make sure that she stays that way. I know Josephine's trial is due to start next week and I can see that she has already started to worry; her anxiety is raising its ugly head again. I am trying to prepare her for the worst-case scenario and we've already discussed the visits, and how we'll fit them around work and the girls. I don't want Shelley to lose her newly found inner contentment. We'll find a way to manage Josephine's absence, however long that is. I won't let her suffer the loss of her mum again.

Shelley

Last night was like the biblical last supper. I knew that today was just the start of the case, and that she'd still be free until sentencing, but I had still wanted everything to be perfect. I did a roast dinner, just like my mum used to make every Sunday. It was important to me. Both Mum and Dad came, obviously the girls and of course Josephine. John even took the night off. In fact, he has taken the whole week. He should have been working on a job, but he wanted to show his support. Mum and him have really bonded.

John has finally been given back his firearms licence, and is no longer confined to a desk job. He's back to doing what he loves. The resentment he once felt towards the Force, what we had both felt, has finally gone. To be honest, I think it went as soon as Jo had got charged, and convicted. He believed that the police had let him down. This whole situation; my arrest, my conviction had made him question his choice of career. However, there was never any other option for John. Policing is in his DNA. It's part of his soul.

Anyway, today is the day, and it's a Gilling-Jones united front. We are all meeting early at the Barristers Chambers.

Josephine

I haven't been able to sleep. I came home early from Shelley's last night. She had cooked a wonderful meal, which I really did enjoy, but I just couldn't settle. I had taken a shoebox around, of old photos to go through with her as we were still playing catch-up. However, we didn't get a chance…. I left them there, hopefully, we'll have some time before I'm sentenced. This is all so cruel. I know this is all my own fault, but I can't help but feel cheated.

Anyway, today is the day. I'm dressed, ready, and on the train. Prepared as much as I can be for my first day in court. I take the now very familiar route to the Barristers Chambers, and as I approach, I see that Shelley and John are waiting outside. As I get closer, Shelley walks at pace towards me. She flings her arms around me and I can feel the sadness in her embrace. It's how a child might feel at their first day of school, when their parent is saying goodbye. I too feel anxious. I am under no illusions as to where my fate lies. I had killed an innocent man. I would be going to prison. My motherly instinct kicks in, and I find myself soothing her. "Right then" I say after I've hugged her tightly back. "Shall we get this started?" I release myself from her and walking past both her and then John, I head straight into the Reception. I immediately spot Mr Bell and Robbie, and then I see a lady that I recognise from when I did work experience all those years ago. Obviously, she was older, we all were, but there was no mistaking her, it was Jenny. She'd helped me with the DX'ing of some documents. I could see that there was also a spark of recognition on her part.

"Jenny isn't it? I can't believe it; you've not changed a bit."

"Yes, it is... Look... Sorry, I recognise you, but I can't think where on earth from..."

I smile. "It's here actually...." Robbie overhears... and he interrupts... "Of course, it's bloody here! She's a client!" Clearly embarrassed, Jenny looks away but then I say ...

"No, not from recently. I did work experience here over 35 years ago. I think you were 17, 18 when I last saw you...."

"Oh, my goodness. Yes!"

"Work Experience!" Robbie pipes up again "Of course!" He says this, as if he's finally put two and two together... Robbie then disappears off, as does Jenny after she has wished me luck with the case.

We, (Shelley, John, and I) are just about to follow Mr Bell into his office, when a young lad approaches. "Can I get you a tea or coffee?" I look at him and I realise that he is clearly there as I was all those years back. I remember only too well how I had made the drinks for the gang who'd killed that young lad, and how disgusted I had been at their nonchalant behaviour - trying their very best to get away with murder.... and here I am, all those years later, doing the exact same thing! Anyway, I thanked him, as did Shelley and John. We all put in our orders and then make our way over to Mr Bell's Glass Office.

It was a very short consultation, if you could even call it that. He said that he would meet us and Isaac over at the court a little later. He just wanted to touch base ahead of the proceedings, but today would just be a day of formalities. The judge would consider the plea, jury selection, etc, etc ... "There is nothing really to worry about" he said. I knew he meant well, but that was all I was doing; I couldn't help but worry.

We left the Chambers shortly afterwards, and made our way over to the court. It was exactly as I had remembered it all those years ago. The Security was a little more vigorous these days, but apart from that nothing had changed. It even smelled the same.

Josephine

The weeks had passed so quickly. On day one I had stood in the dock and the Clerk had read out the charges. It was decided by the Judge that although there was evidence of my defence, he wasn't sure it was sufficient on the balance of probabilities, so he decided that we would be proceeding to trial. He did however, direct that the charge of manslaughter was to be added to the indictment.

I sat in the dock, day after day as the Prosecution painted me as a vengeful killer. Driven only by hate. They questioned my delay in coming forward, my very deliberate, and methodical disposal of the body. They even put their own medical expert on the stand to try to counter the findings and diagnosis from Dr Julius. Dr Julius was the Psychiatrist who'd originally confirmed my PTSD diagnosis. She provided the evidence in chief, that on the day of Joseph's death, having seen who I believed was my previous attacker, and the fact that I was at the exact location, it had meant that I suffered a catastrophic flashback. A flashback so severe that I had thought that I were under immediate attack. The PTSD had triggered a mental disorder that had substantially impaired my ability to form a rational judgement, and exercise any sort of self-control. My diary entries had been crucial in painting the scene, and had given credence to her theory. Dr Julius after the two hours of giving evidence said, "It is in my expert opinion that the unresolved trauma, resulting from the events in the accuses childhood, were wholly contributory in causing her to act in the way she did. Her actions at that time and immediately afterwards were driven by an abnormal and out of control belief at that point."

My defence team painted me as the principal victim, and I had sobbed throughout. I gave my own account of the events leading up to Colin Joseph's death, and of course, the prosecution tried to undermine me. Mr

Bell, however, he used a cross-section of witnesses from the entirety of my life to support the account that I had given. Imogen; my boss at the Library said that I was a model employee. I did everything I was told to do, including studying for a Masters Degree. She highlighted the fact that I was fearful of ever doing anything wrong. She mentioned my inability to form any real close bonds, stating that I'd never once gone to any social event. "She just preferred her own company; I think she felt safer that way." She recalled a time when I'd broken down very uncharacteristically, and I had sobbed in her arms. She could not remember what had triggered it, but she put it down to some sort of inner turmoil. She had absolutely no idea that I had been raped as a child, abandoned my baby, and then tried to take my own life. She recounted the day that I went missing. "She collapsed at work quite unexpectedly. I called an ambulance. They checked her over and I sent her home. However, she didn't come back. That's why I reported her missing."

Other witnesses, they also included a parishioner at the church who knew me after the event, and a university tutor. They both described me as introvert, vulnerable and troubled. All except the barmaid from my dad's local, she remembered me before it all happened. Describing me as "a happy and sociable little girl, you could clearly see the close bond that she had with her dad." The retired nurse who'd looked after me when I'd tried to kill myself - she had said how mentally and physically ill I had been. She stated that she had noted the recent pregnancy, and had assumed that I had miscarried. She also advised that I'd been released into my mother's care, and that any further support was down to the Local Authorities' Social Services. "I would have completed the paperwork, but it was the 1980's and we didn't have the same checks that we have today..."

As well as painting me as the victim, Mr Bell knew that he had to recognise the tragedy of Joseph's death. He took the time to highlight my obvious remorse, which of course he very cleverly weaved in throughout.

"She tried to do the right thing…" He had focused on my attendance at the Central Police Station in the March. The fact that the police had failed to follow up on my written confession, and my provision of the murder weapon.

"They did nothing. In fact, they actively concealed it!"

He countered the Prosecution's accusations that I fled abroad to prevent being held accountable. Instead, his narrative focused on the vulnerability of a 14-year-old girl, in whose mind I'd temporarily gotten lost in.

"She was unsure of whom to turn to… I ask you to consider this…. as a child when you do something wrong, do you rush to own up, or do you run away and hide for fear of punishment? We have heard of the accused strict Catholic upbringing, the sudden loss of her father. We have heard how she was failed by the church, her own mother, Social Services, the list goes on......"

".... She accepts that she did wrong, she accepts that had she not been overtaken by fear, and the very real flashback from the earlier trauma; this terrible incident would never have occurred" .... "And let us not forget that as soon as she was of sound mind again, she returned to the UK and handed herself in."

The Prosecution in summing up said the diagnosis of PTSD was nothing more than a lie, and that I'd only sought it, in support of my narrative. They tried their best to demonstrate how I'd gone to great lengths to hide what I'd done. That I'd lived independently for years, and that I had been able to achieve in life;

significantly unaffected. Holding down a career at the Library, and even undertaking complex studies. All of which was recognised by my defence, but the fact still remained that I had an undiagnosed condition, that even I was not aware of. Therefore, I could not be held accountable for an involuntary act. In his closing argument, Mr Bell finished with…

"If you are going to deliver a guilty verdict, you need to be absolutely sure, and in no doubt, that she had been in control that day, and that she purposely did this terrible act, consciously and without suffering from any abnormality of the mind…."

After a very long, and exhausting three weeks, the Judge finally gave his directions to the Jury. We were all excused and all I could do then was wait.

DS Rachel Cooper

As the Officer in the Case, I had obviously attended the court every single day. As predicted, they made her out to be the victim, and not Joseph. Everyone seemed to have forgotten about poor old Colin. This recluse of a man who was desperately lonely, and had met a horrific end.

Even I, when I first interviewed her had been consumed by her story. A story that she religiously stuck to in court. She never once wavered from her prepared statement, and she was credible when the Prosecution tried to undermine her account. Maybe I had got this all wrong. Maybe she hadn't been responsible for those other deaths.

Manslaughter had also been put on the table, so it was obvious where it was all leading. At his summing up the

Judge, a very imposing man, he practically told the Jury what to do.

"If you are satisfied that the defendant murdered Mr Joseph, and you are sure of guilt, then nothing less will do. However, if after considering ALL *(he emphasised this)* of the evidence; Medical Reports, Witness Testimonies, including that of the defendant, and you are not sure; the verdict must be not guilty."

I think the Jury deliberated for all of 5 minutes, and even that probably included a loo break. They gave a verdict of not guilty to murder, but they did find her guilty of manslaughter by reason of diminished responsibility.

The sentencing hearing is set for next week.

One week later

John

We are back at the Chambers, and all of us are crowded into a very grand meeting-room, Shelley, Josephine, Myself. Isaac, Robbie, Mr Bell, and the rest of the Defence Team. Each one of us clutching a champagne flute, full to the top with a very fine vintage Taittinger.

We were celebrating and rather surprisingly, it was Robbie who made the toast.

"Today, we made history. There is now caselaw ***R V Gilling*** that clearly shows PTSD as a credible defence to murder. Josephine, this is a landmark case, and I want to be the first to congratulate you on your continued freedom. May all of your past troubles be firmly behind you. I also want to congratulate William and his team. This case has been ground-breaking and it has put Clarks Court firmly back on the map. The phone has been ringing off the hook this afternoon with people wanting to put business our way.   So, I thank you all for that!

Now Josephine; I know that I said we would give you your final bill on conclusion…Well, I have spoken to our very own Mr John Allott Abrahams QC, and he has waived it. It is his belief that it's payment for the work experience that you did for us back in the 1980's. By all accounts, he was very impressed by your work…"

This raises a smile… "Now everyone, please raise your glass…… To Josephine and the best possible outcome!"

Everyone raises their glass and then the room erupts into conversation.

I turn to Shelley. "Are you OK?"

She nods her head at my question…. "Yes. I can't believe it's all over. How did she even get a suspended sentence?"

"Well, it was obviously meant to be. He has considered all the evidence… Think about it. She was remorseful, previously of good character, definitely no history of violence…. People are only really imprisoned to protect the public. She's been assessed, and is now shown of sound mind. She's having counselling to deal with her past issues… What risk is she?"

"Well, I was of previously good character. I didn't have a history of violence and they still locked me up!"

"Yes darling, but you showed no remorse!"

"Are you kidding me? No remorse, of course I showed no remorse! I didn't bloody do it!!"

"Yes, I know, I know! I'm playing with you, calm down!"

"Yes…. I know, sorry, I think the bubbles have gone to my head. I always did get a bit bolshie on this stuff…"

"It's good news though isn't it?"

"Oh god, John, it's the best. I had only just started to get to know her... I don't think I could have coped."

"Well, she just needs to keep up this charade (I say jokingly) for another three years and she's home and dry."

"Oh, John! Stop it!!" Shelley says laughing, a little uncontrollably... The champers has definitely got to her!

Josephine

"I don't really know how to thank you. I was convinced that I was going to prison. I still can't believe it."

"Ah Josephine, it was the only 'just' outcome. You have been punished enough." Isaac replies in his soothing tones as always.

"Anyway, what are you going to do now?"

"Um, I'm not sure really, I suppose catch up on the 40 years, that I have missed out on with my daughter..."

"It sounds perfect. Look ... I need to catch up with William, but if you ever need anything, I am always here for you." At this, and rather unusually for me, I felt an uncontrollable urge to hug Isaac. His mannerisms had reminded me so much of my dad. I threw my arms around him, nearly knocking his glass from his hand... He returned the hug but it was a little awkward.

"Thank you!" I say. "Thank you for everything."

"It's OK." He pats my back one hand-idly, still holding on to his glass, and then he moves off towards William.

I'm left stood in the middle of the room, alone. There is so much buzz, so much energy. I still cannot believe what has just happened to me. Did I really just get away with murder?

John

I get back to the room after visiting the gents. I don't know about Shelley and the champers going to her head, but I definitely feel a little jaded myself. The puff-pastry canapés' that have been laid out on the table are a lovely gesture, but I would need to eat hundreds of them to counteract the booze. I'd forgotten just how susceptible I was. I think the last time that I drank the good stuff was actually at our wedding.

I can see that Shelley and her mother are in full conversation, so I don't interrupt them. Robbie then approaches me. "Good result isn't it!" He slurs his words a little, so even he is a lightweight.
"Yes, absolutely brilliant!" I reply as If we were discussing the weekend fixtures, and not my mother-in-law having just got away with murder.
"Do you know what?" Robbie continues. "I'm 71 this year and I know I could retire, but I really don't want to.

It's cases like this that make it all worthwhile. We do so much work where you question your ethics, your morality, but this case, yes although tragic for the chap who died; I know this really was the only right result... Do you see what I'm saying?"

I nod my head... "I know exactly what you mean. I'm a copper, have been for over twenty years. I see things very black and white normally, but with the life she's had, there is definitely some grey to be considered."

"You are so right. Don't get me wrong, she has a strength of character... We had absolutely no inkling, when she was this keen work-experience kid. It took me a while to place her when she first came here with Isaac... She used to be blonde you know? But those blue eyes... absolutely unforgettable. I remember now, she took a real keen interest in a case that we had at the time. Briggs was his name, suspected paedophile. We got him acquitted. Poor bastard, the mud must have stuck, as he only went and topped himself at Beachy Head. I only really remember him because he didn't pay his bill... Ah here they come, they could be sisters, couldn't they?" Robbie says this as he wobbles off towards the buffet, leaving me stood there, between Shelley and her mum.

Josephine

Life has pretty much returned to as it was before. I'm actually back working at the Library. Backroom stuff but that suits me. Imogen has been so supportive throughout all of this. I feel in a way that I owe her my life. Her testimony at my trial was heartfelt, and I am sure that it helped to sway the jury.

I'm also a regular around at Shelley and John's. I even help out with the school run when I'm not working. The girls call me Nana Jo Jo. It's wonderful seeing their beaming faces on the way out of the school gate. I'm around there tomorrow afternoon actually, and we are finally going to go through that shoebox, that I had popped around there before the start of the trial. I cannot wait to share all of my old memories with her and those gorgeous little grandchildren of mine.

John

I'm late for a briefing. I run up the stairs and slam straight into a very pretty brunette.

"Sorry, I didn't see you there…"

"Ah, it's OK, no harm done…." She looks at me… "Err, John isn't it?"

"Yes… that's right, sorry, rubbish with names…."

"It's Kate, Kate Groves…"

"Oh. OK…" *I still don't know who she is*… She continues…

"You don't actually know me… but I know your wife and her mother…"

"Ah right…."

"Yes, I've actually been trying to get hold of Josephine, but her mobile and landline aren't connecting."

"Yes, she's got new numbers; the press had managed to get hold of her old ones. They wouldn't leave her alone."

"That makes sense…"

"Anything that I can help with?"

"Well, I'm the OIC on her rape case. I really need to let her know that it's going to be discontinued."

"Discontinued? Why?"

"Well… He's dead."

"Who is? Jacobs?"

"Yes, I found out last week. Apparently, he was found partially buried in the Dunes. Single stab wound to the chest."

"Really? When did this happen?"

"They are working on the theory that it was 8-9 months ago. He'd had a call on his mobile, and he left the office suddenly. He'd been working on some high-profile installation over there. He was an engineer or something. Anyway, he'd even got a protection detail, paid for by the client but he had given them the slip. The client was some wealthy Sheik. Apparently, they'd received some sort of threat... They are working on the theory that his murder must be connected in some way… So, unfortunately, we won't be arresting him."

"Well… No… OK. Do you want me to tell her, or I can give you her number?"

"What's best? Do you want me to?" *I think for a moment.*

"No, it's fine, I'll do it. I need to tell Shelley anyway."

"Ok, thank you. Look, let her know that if she wants to know more, to give me a call."

"Yep, will do."

I make my way into the Briefing Room, obviously even later than I was before. I make my apologies…. My head is buzzing.

Shelley

Mum and I have been sat on the lounge-room floor for most of the afternoon. The contents of her shoebox, once full of old photos, now strewn all over the place. We get on so well, we really are more like sisters. I think that this is because of the small age gap. John had called and said that he would pick up the girls on his way home, so that I didn't need to rush out and get them. It was all the excuse that I needed, and so I'd got a bottle of white from the fridge, and we were already well into it...

"Oh my god! Look at your hair... and what are you wearing?" We are both laughing at the photos of Mum. "You look just like me as a kid, only I had better dress sense!"
"Oi cheeky..." Mum responded... "Remember who you are talking to... You're not too old to be put across my

knee, you know!" Josephine puts on her best Irish accent... presumably to sound like her own mother...

The front door springs open and in come Maggie and Heidi... "In here!" I shout...
"Come and see some funny photos of Nana Jo Jo." The girls come in, followed by John... "Having fun, are we?" John says this, pointing to the half bottle of wine on the coffee table, and the now empty glasses.
"Yes actually...." I respond.
"Oh, my goodness! Look at that one... What has happened to your fringe?"
"What do you mean?... It was windy... That's me and Dad at the very top of Beachy Head... I loved all those holidays, such fond memories... God! I've not been there for at least 20 years... We should go..."

I look over at John, and he looks like he's seen a ghost.
"You ok love?... Sorry, I should have asked... Do you want a glass? I can get you one."

"No, it's fine, I've just remembered something that I forgot to do at work. Are you OK with the girls if I pop out?"

"Yes, no problem, so long as you're OK?"

John leans over to kiss me. He'd normally have kissed Mum goodbye too, but this time he doesn't. He just turns and leaves. Whatever it is, it must be serious.

John

I get straight back into the car, and I go to drive off. It will take me at least 40 minutes at this time of the day to get back to the Station. I feel sick and I don't think I can wait that long. I need to know now. I make the call and she picks up immediately.

"Oh, Hi John, I didn't expect you to call... Everything, all right?"

"Yes, everything is fine. Look Rachel, those historic cases, the ones that you thought Josephine was linked to... What were the names?"

"Oh hang-on, I'm in the office. I'll just check. You'd think I'd remember...." She fumbles about, and I can hear static on the line...

"Yep, here they are... Pike, Frost and Briggs."

"Briggs? Are you sure?"

"Yes, Paul Briggs."

I go silent.

"Why what's this about? John, why do you want to know?"

I can't answer her...

"Look, I've got to go..."

With that, I have ended the call. I know what I need to do.

I get out of the car and I walk straight back into the house. Shelley, Heidi, Maggie, and Josephine, are all in fits of giggles, sitting on the lounge floor. They don't even notice me. I have never seen Shelley so happy, so relaxed. I take a deep breath and I go to speak, but I can't. I walk away from the doorway, and I go into the kitchen. I make my way over to the fridge and take out a beer. I open it and take a sip whilst leaning against the counter. I can feel my back pocket vibrate. It's my phone. I take it out and look at the caller ID. It's Rachel. I think for a second or so about answering it, but then I reject her call.

I think back to the events of the past years and months, and there and then, I decide for the sake of Shelley and my family; black and white is no longer my colour. From now on I choose grey.

THE END.

Find out what happens next in **ABSOLUTION**. This is available as a paperback from Amazon or to download from the Kindle Store.

This is a work of fiction. Names, characters, businesses, places, events, locales, and incidents are either the products of the author's imagination or used in a fictitious manner. Any resemblance to actual persons, living or dead, or actual events is purely coincidental.

A note from the author...

Thank you so much for taking the time to read my book. I really appreciate your support.

If you liked what you read, or even if you didn't, please feel free to leave me some constructive feedback.

If you did enjoy this however, and want to read another book written by me.... why not try the next book in the Rachel Cooper Series? All three books are available to download as e-books on Kindle or as paperback editions on Amazon.

Body in the Wood, Hunted & Absolution.

If you want to keep up to date with my latest projects, or you just want to know more about me, why not follow me on Amazon, or visit my website

www.kecullenwriter.co.uk

Printed in Great Britain
by Amazon